Hush Money

A TALENT CHRONICLES NOVEL

SUSAN BISCHOFF

ACKNOWLEDGEMENTS

The author wishes to give a grateful shout-out to the following people:

~To Kait Nolan, fantastic writer, dearest friend, and invaluable partner in crime, for brainstorming, cajoling, editing, finding Joss's face, hand-holding, honesty, fight scene choreography, technical and emotional support, and…I could go on all day. Thanks for being absolutely the best critique partner anyone could ask for. You are THE person who made this book possible.

~To Zoe Winters (Zoe Who?), for inspiration, answers to a million questions, outrageous laughs, beta reading, and did I mention inspiration? Thanks for being your kick-ass self, bitches.

~To Amanda, Victoria, Megan, Valerie, Alex, Christel, Brandi, Heather, and Mom for beta reading, enthusiasm, and typo-corrections.

~To Robin Ludwig, Robin Ludwig Design Inc., for stepping in and putting together a wonderful cover for me, very quickly. Thanks for all your attention and beautiful work.

~To my daughter, Briar Rose, for putting up with my divided attention or lack thereof. And to my parents, for occasionally entertaining her so I could write.

~To my husband, Les, for being the kind of guy all my heroes aspire to be, and for putting up with a lot. Trust me, a *lot*.

~And lastly, to Mr. Stokas, my favorite teacher ever, for telling me to write.

ABOUT THE TALENTS

The world of the Talent Chronicles was born out of my love of both superheroes and romance. I've always been drawn to the characters whose supernatural abilities set them apart from everyone else. Some are loved by all and known by none, some are woefully misunderstood and mistreated by those they serve. Traditionally, the life of the super-powered being seems to be one destined for loneliness, and yet so deserving of a happily ever after.

That's what I wanted to give them.

They call their abilities Talents, and that's what they call themselves as well. Talents are people born with supernatural powers, feared by the population at large. Possession of an "unregistered ability" has become illegal, and those who are discovered are forcibly removed to government-run research facilities.

And so the Talents try, as best they can, to keep their abilities secret–some more successfully than others. For some, keeping that secret begins to define who they are. And that's where **Hush Money** begins.

Hush Money is the first story to be completed in their world. A second story, tentatively titled *Heroes 'Til Curfew*, is currently in the works. I hope you'll join me in their future adventures. For up-to-date release and contact information, please visit me at http://susan-bischoff.com.

CHAPTER 1

Joss

I already knew it had happened again.

Not like I'm psychic, not really, but you don't have to have any special mental Talent to see the signs…if you're paying attention.

Stacy Scarpelli had had her hand in the air for, like, five minutes. Eventually she was doing that thing where you lean one elbow on the desk, and your other elbow in your hand, like you're going to collapse from the exhaustion of trying to get the teacher's attention. But the teacher was paying attention. She was paying a lot of attention to checking off names on the roll; or supposedly taking roll, but totally not looking at that whole side of the room where Stacy was flinging her hand limply about on her wrist.

And leave it to Stacy to be so wrapped up in Stacy that she didn't notice how quiet it was this morning in first period English and how everyone just kind of sat there. The whispering would start later, as the shock wore off. Later, people would be saying how long they'd suspected, and how much they'd never really liked Krista anyway. But just then we were all looking around at each other and wondering who else was keeping secrets, and who would be the next one to disappear.

Ms. Carter looked up and set her pencil down very carefully on her desk, lining it up precisely next to her planner, and finally raised her eyes to Stacy.

"Yes, Stacy?"

"You assigned me Krista to be my partner for the project. And it's not like I wanted to leave it to the last minute, but she was always later later later, you know? And

1

finally I said we gotta get together this weekend, and we were supposed to meet on Saturday morning before my tennis lesson? So I waited and waited for her, but she didn't show up, and I *had* to get to my lesson, right? And then I called her house after, but no one answered. No one answered all weekend, and now she's not even here today, and I don't know if she did any work at all on it. I did some, but I was kind of waiting to find out what she had, you know, compare notes, because there was no point in us doing the same thing, right? But I couldn't 'cause she wouldn't answer her phone and then I didn't know what to do, and I was going nuts all weekend trying to get a hold of her—"

"Ok, Stacy. See me after class and we'll work something out."

"I mean, I don't think I should be penalized because she was too busy to work on the project. Which she probably didn't anyway, which is probably why she didn't show up Saturday, and dodged my calls all weekend, and she's probably ditching school today so—"

"She's not ditching; she's just gone."

All eyes slid toward Dylan. He sat sideways in his chair, the back of his leather jacket against the chalkboard along the side wall, long legs stretched out in front of him, his expression unreadable.

In the seat behind him, Marco tipped back in his chair. "NIAC hauled her off." His voice was laced with the kind of satisfaction over other people's tragedies that made me think about his chair tipping too far and his skull bouncing off the linoleum.

Ms. Carter glanced nervously around the room. I felt bad for her. How's a teacher supposed to handle this subject? Encourage open discussion? Answer questions? Should we all share our feelings about the fact that we were never going to see Krista Pace again? It just seemed to me that the faculty probably knew about it earlier. Hell, the *National Institutes for Ability Control* probably sent out some kind of official letter to the school, wouldn't you think? Our regular teacher should have been there for support and guidance instead of leaving the poor student-teacher to the wolves. But then, what would Mr. Krause have done differently?

"[cough]Freak![cough]"

"Shut up, Marco." Dylan continued to bounce his pencil's eraser on the desk and examine his boot-tops.

"Why, did you and freak-girl have something goin' on? Need a new date for Homecoming now that NIAC's locked her up?"

Enquiring minds want to know. My mind was particularly interested, unfortunately.

"Thanks, but you're not my type," Dylan sneered back at his friend.

"Ok, people, that's enough," Ms. Carter finally gathered the courage to enter the conversation. "The topic of Krista Pace is off-limits in this class. If you have questions regarding her disap— If you have questions, you may take them to Assistant Principal Sims—on your own time. Meanwhile, I believe we have some oral presentations to hear today. Stacy, you can see me after class about your project. Who wants to go first?"

Personally, I think the school system is pretty messed up. I mean, if Krista had been hit by a bus or if she'd died of some terminal disease she'd been bravely fighting in secret for years, there'd be announcements, a moment of silence over the PA, maybe a memorial assembly. And we'd probably have some kind of shrine where people would leave pictures of Krista with flowers and little teddy bears and stuff like that. Out front somewhere, where the TV news cameras could see it clearly, and give it lots of attention, and call it a "makeshift memorial" fifteen times a freakin' day. Like you've got to spend $5000 on a friggin' stone pillar or fountain with an engraved placard on it because anything else is just "makeshift."

But I digress.

Maybe we'd have grief counseling to talk about how she was just ripped from our lives, and we would never be able to say goodbye. We'd talk about how we felt that she'd never told us about this horrible disease she had, and if we'd known we would have been nicer to her, and now we'd never have the chance.

Because really, Krista was never coming back. And what she had was a lot like a disease. Something she was born with, something that couldn't be cured, something very, very bad.

What Krista Pace had was a Talent.

* * *

Joss

God save us from guidance counselors…

I swiped my sweaty palm down the front of the vintage army field jacket I always wore before grabbing the doorknob and letting myself into the guidance department office. I handed my hall pass to the woman at the desk inside the door whose name I'd never bothered to learn.

I absolutely hated it here.

"Jocelyn. Yes, Mr. Dobbs is waiting for you. Go on in."

I turned away and moved to the door, thinking belatedly that I should have said thank you. Eye contact, a smile, thank you. But I never was any good at that politeness stuff. I was a lot better at the being quiet and melting into the background stuff. Having someone call up my Math teacher, being singled out and told to report to the guidance office while the rest of the class waited to get on with the being bored—er, educated? It really messed with my whole *don't notice me* program.

I was already on edge from that morning—because of the whole Krista thing—and this just made me twitchy. It didn't help that I knew exactly why Dobbs had called me in here.

I did not want to talk about it.

"Joss." He shuffled some papers into a folder, closed it. "Come on in. Have a seat."

I took the seat across from the desk without speaking, keeping my messenger bag on my shoulder and my notebook to my chest. I kept my expression blank, rather than overtly sullen, but Dobbs prided himself on the whole reading the body language thing and my message should be clear.

He took off his glasses and drew the side of his hand along the bridge of his nose as he set them down on the desk. In a moment he would pick them back up and put them on again, because he needed them to see. But his ritual of taking them off, setting them down... that was his way of saying he was serious, yet caring, concerned, and open-minded.

See, I could do body language too.

"So....how's it going?" he asked, dragging out the question.

"Ok."

He picked up his glasses and put them back on. "You've heard about Krista."

I didn't say anything. It wasn't a question, and what was I supposed to say, anyway? It wasn't like the school had any kind of official stance on this stuff. They must cooperate in whatever investigations went on, but they never made, like, statements to the press or anything. There was nothing for me to quote or agree with.

"I thought you might have some feelings you'd like to talk about."

You thought that? Really? Are you new here? "No, not really."

"Joss, I know this must bring up some issues for you, feelings I don't think you've ever really dealt with. About Emily."

The name was like an execute command, automatically flashing a series of images across my brain that started out like a real estate or life insurance commercial. Little girls playing, laughing, holding hands, dancing in sprinklers, birthday parties, sharing secrets, fire, screaming, end of reel.

I jammed the playback to a stop before it could loop, forced my eyes from the stupid cartoon character on Dobbs's tie, and actually met his eyes. I shoved the discomfort at the personal contact aside with the rest of my feelings and made myself cold. "Emily moved away. Lots of kids have childhood friends who move away. It's sad at the time, but it's not, like, traumatic or anything."

Dobbs waited for me to say more. I figured it was safer to let him steer the conversation rather than take the lead and risk saying the wrong thing. These counselor types could be so tricksy. It wasn't my first time in his office, and I knew he liked to try to read into things people said.

"But Emily didn't just move away. A child's parent might get a job in another town, they break the news, and there's weeks, maybe months, of house-hunting, packing— a period to adjust before the actual move. It wasn't like that with Emily. One day the two of you were joined at the hip, running up and down the block, picking the dandelions from everyone's yards...Then all of a sudden she was just...gone."

I continued to hold the eye contact, because to drop it now would be a show of weakness, like I had something to hide. I did a mental check and loosened my fingers on my notebook a little before he noticed my white-knuckled grip.

Dobbs had lived a few houses down and across the street for as long as I could remember. He was the kind of neighbor who waved if he saw you, but didn't walk over to chat. He didn't mind if you went through his gate after a lost ball or a Frisbee, but he never invited you to swim in his pool. In all the years of casual neighboring, he'd never once tried to talk to me about Emily. But since my first day in high school, he'd used any excuse to drag me into his office to try to discuss my *feelings* on the subject.

Why was I suddenly of interest? Was it just because talking to me became part of his job? Or was there something in that folder he didn't know from just living in the same neighborhood? Had someone told him to ask questions?

Get a grip.

"And then there was the fire…" he continued.

"I told you I don't remember any fire."

"The last time we spoke I suggested you discuss it with your parents."

"I did. I asked my mom about it. She didn't know what I was talking about." This was a planned answer. If Dobbs went to my mom, she would explain that she and dad felt it was best that I wasn't reminded about the incident.

His eyes narrowed as he mulled over that response. I could see the wheels turning behind his pale eyes, realizing that my parents would probably not be open to the idea of him helping their daughter achieve any kind of emotional breakthrough.

Point scored for Team Marshall.

"Hmmm, well…. If you're sure there's nothing you'd like to discuss…"

"Nothing I can think of."

"Don't forget to have Ms. Clark give you a hall pass."

During class the girls' bathrooms were usually deserted, but not the one closest to the guidance offices. That one was too close to the gym, and chances were it would be occupied by those whose decisions to skip gym were more whim than plan, and hadn't come up with any better option. So I'd had to shuffle along two hallways and up a flight of stairs before finding a quiet stall where I could take a few shuddering breaths and try to pull myself back together.

God, I hated Dobbs, the supercilious bastard. *And then there was the fire...* I mocked him in my head, using my best idiot voice. *Yeah, now that you mention it, I do suddenly want to talk about it. And, you know, I feel so close to you now that I feel like I can share my secret.*

As if. Asshat.

Thing was, I could be pissed all I wanted to, but that didn't seem to be stopping the movie in my head, the feelings of dread as I watched it play out, knowing I couldn't stop the little girls from their stupid plan. It didn't stop me from reliving the terror as things spun out of control, or the equally worse fear in the aftermath as we waited to see what would happen. As the unthinkable happened. As everything changed.

I felt wetness on my face and muttered a curse, leaning down for some toilet paper. But of course it was empty. I banged the back of my head on the door as I rummaged in my bag with one hand. I had to get a grip on myself. *No better way to get noticed in school than to walk around looking like I've been cry—*

Still clutching the oversized notebook in my arms, I fumbled the bunch of stuff I'd pulled out of my bag to sort through for a tissue. Instinctively, I reached out with my mind and caught everything. The objects hovered in the air above the bowl: a pen, a scrunchie, a few crumpled bills, and the tissue.

I held them there a moment, feeling in my head those fragile, invisible strings between each object and my mind. It would hardly take any effort at all to open up my bag, tug at those imaginary strings, and float everything right back in. But in my mind I could hear my dad's voice saying, *"The best way to seem normal is to be normal."*

I put out my hand, grasped the crumpled piece of Kleenex, and let the other things go. The scrunchie bounced off the seat and landed on the floor, the pen and the money hit the water. I put my boot to the handle and flushed.

Be normal, I thought. *It's just that easy.*

CHAPTER 2

Dylan

"Dylan, bum a smoke."

"No, man, I quit."

"What, again?" Marco half whined, like I'd made the decision just to inconvenience him.

"Hey, Marco, I gotcha." Jeff took a last drag and passed his cigarette to Marco before reaching into his jacket for another.

"God damn, when is this rain ever going to stop?" I turned up my collar when a drop rolled off the slight overhang and snaked its way down my neck. I pressed my back against the wall with the other guys and kept my eyes open for Assistant Principle Sims.

"When it snows. So what is it now? It's a little late to start a college fund." There was something about Marco. Everything needed an explanation with him, even something as simple as me giving up cigarettes for the umpteenth time.

I'm starting a getaway fund in case they come for me next. "I'm savin' up for an ark."

"Oh, well that'll work for you. The world covered in water and it's just you and a boatload of sheep," Jeff snarked.

"Jealous much?"

Marco snorted, ready to let it go, and Eric said, to no one in particular, "Bet Krista wishes she'd prepared for a rainy day."

Eric was often the quiet one, and maybe it was all that observation he did that made him seem too damned perceptive sometimes.

"That freak bitch. I knew there was something off about her."

Yeah, Marco, you knew it from the first time she told you no. "Would you give it a rest?"

"What's with you?" Marco snapped.

"What's with *you?*" I shot back. "I'm just tired of your bullshit, that's all."

"You're always like this when they take someone," Jeff complained.

I looked across Marco to where Jeff was avoiding eye contact with me. "Like what?"

"I don't know. All, like, morose and shit. Get over it."

"Aw, leave him alone," Marco said, clapping a hand on my shoulder and giving it a shake. It looked like a friendly gesture from the outside, but it was only the extraordinary strength of Marco's grip on my shoulder that kept me from falling over. Fortunately, I had learned to tuck my chin to my chest to avoid having the back of my head crack against the wall behind me. "You know he's been trying that sensitivity thing. How's that workin' for you?"

"Obviously he has to beat the chicks back with a stick," Jeff sneered.

"The bell's gonna ring." *And save me from you idiots I call my friends,* I thought as I pushed away from the wall and headed for the fire door we'd propped open.

"Yo, wait up," Marco said, catching my arm, propelling me ahead and away from the other guys. "I've got an idea about this weekend. We'll talk about it later."

My stomach clenched. This was exactly the conversation I wanted to avoid and really couldn't put off much longer. Marco and his expectations were going to land me in jail. Or worse. "This weekend? You really think that's a good idea? I mean what with Krista and all?"

"Yeah, maybe you're right. Damn, I could use the cash. That's ok, though, because I've got something else coming up. Something big." He clapped me on the shoulder again and this time there was no show of strength, just the connection. "What would I do without you, buddy? You're always thinkin'. Always got my back."

Yeah. You bet.

* * *

Joss

How bad does it have to get before I can call it the worst day ever?

First Krista, then freakin' Dobbs, and then Mr. Hanson. He'd cornered me after Chem to talk to me about my lousy performance on the latest test. My dad was going to have a fit about that. Bad grades, like outstanding grades, draw attention. A solid B average is the thing to aim for. Anyway, the impromptu summary of the covalent-whatever deal—which I still didn't get—had delayed me in my usual pre-lunch routine, and gotten me nabbed by a hall monitor. Do Not Pass Go, do not sneak up to your usual hideout, go directly to the Fifth Circle of Hell, otherwise known as the cafeteria.

It's not like I'd never been to the cafeteria before. I used to have to eat there when I was a freshman, for a few very long months, anyway, before I figured out how to avoid it. I remembered now that the best caf' strategy was to take your lunch with you to the class before so you could race down there, as inconspicuously as possible, and claim an empty table. It was ok for later arrivals to sit at your table, which they might do, crowding together on the opposite side like you have a disease, but whatever. As long as you got there first, you didn't have to ask to sit at

13

anyone else's table—and risk being told no, because what's more humiliating than that? Sometimes people would just take all the chairs from your table and carry them off to other tables, and that's sort of embarrassing too, but not as bad if you don't let it get to you and remind yourself that lunching alone is a valid lifestyle choice. On the whole, though, the cafeteria is a bad scene and to be avoided whenever possible.

So there I was, standing in the doorway, taking a quick scan of the room and scoping things out. I still had a notebook and textbook for Chem, so I moved them to carry them under my arm. Because you can't be holding books in front of you like a shield. It's way girly and makes people think you're scared. Posturing is very important in the wild; watch a few documentaries, you'll see.

I couldn't spend too much time hovering, because that was only going to draw attention, so I just plunged in and hoped for the best. The caf' was friggin' chaos as usual. I think I have a low tolerance for chaos. I kept scanning, knowing that I wasn't going to find an empty table, but hoped maybe I'd see an empty space near someone I was at least on speaking terms with, and could come up with some burning question I had to ask. It's hard to look around for such a specific situation while still trying to avoid eye contact, let me tell you.

And then I saw it. There were two chairs just standing there in the corner against the wall. One was pushed all the way into the corner and facing out into the room, the other facing the corner. I could sit with my back to the room, put my boots up on the one in the corner, prop my textbook up on my knees, and pretend like I just had to absorb some chemistry knowledge. Perfect.

Except for the fact that I had to pass Marco's table, and I was so excited about the chairs that I didn't even notice him until my books flew out from under my arm and hit the floor. I think I knew what happened before I even saw him. Some kind of *prey recognizes predator right before it gets eaten* kind of thing.

"Oops," he said, in that obnoxious, *I so meant to do that* way.

I had to squat down to pick up the books, because of course papers went flying out of my notebook when it landed. Thankfully they didn't go far and I didn't actually have to go crawling under tables for them.

"Sorry about that, Joss."

"Sure."

"Surprised to see you here."

I didn't answer. I had some answers in my head; it just seemed better to keep my mouth shut and move on.

"You never come here for lunch. Are you meeting your girlfriend? Why don't you bring her over? Jeff, get a couple chairs for Joss and her new girlfriend."

See, this is a thing between Marco and me, and it's really unpleasant. When we were freshmen, I guess he had this thing for me, because he asked me to the Homecoming dance. And he kept bugging me to go out with him for like a week or something until I finally had to get nasty with him so he'd leave me alone. Not like insulting his masculinity nasty, just, you know, the *I don't like you* truth of it. I don't know why we have to think that telling the truth is being mean, but sometimes I'm powerless against my socialization, what can I tell you? Anyway, ever since then, he'd been on this *You must be a lesbian* thing, because I guess that's the only way it made sense for him that I wouldn't just fall at his feet. Mostly I just avoided him.

Which is what I tried to do at that point by standing up with my books and taking a step away from the table, except that he caught my arm.

"Let me go, Marco."

"Or what, you'll get your girlfriend over here to kick my ass?"

Jeff chuckled at that, and I knew that would only make Marco feel like he had an audience so he'd be more into hassling me. I couldn't help but glance over at Dylan. Because I'm an idiot. He was at the other end of the table with Eric. They had their noses stuck in a car magazine and didn't seem to notice what was going on.

I think Marco noticed because his eyes narrowed at me, and my stomach rolled. Marco can be really mean, and what's more, he's not that typical big, stupid bully *as seen on TV*. He's smart enough to come up with the kind of stuff that really hurts. Stuff that sticks forever.

"Joss, where have you been? Come on. Lunch is half over."

What the...? I turned my head—Marco still had my arm—and Kat was standing there. I wouldn't even say I had a speaking relationship with Kat. She'd said "hi" to me last month, and one time in the locker room she'd asked to borrow lotion from me which of course I didn't have. She was new to Fairview High this year, and I had to wonder what she was doing, and if she realized how stupid it was to get on Marco's bad side.

"Kat? You and *Kat*?"

"She and *Kat* need to study for Chem," Kat said in her sassy way, with a quick glance at my books. "Because I just don't get it. So...if you'd just turn her loose, I'd sure appreciate it."

Kat is pretty. There's just no other way to see it. She's got this gorgeous café au lait skin, light green eyes, and lots of dark brown curls. When she turned that pretty smile on Marco, I felt his grip go slack.

Then I, being an idiot as I might have mentioned, glanced at Dylan again, to see if he'd noticed Kat's smile. Which he had, and was now paying attention to the drama.

I wondered how many more people were, now that Kat was there.

"Chemistry. I'll bet there's some chemistry goin' on there. I'd like to see some of that action. Maybe the three of us—"

"Marco, honey, I'm gonna have to wreck your fantasy and tell you that not only are Joss and I not involved with each other, and not only are we both straight—which you'd think any *straight guy* would realize—but I would do her and half the guys at this table before I would even let you watch me change my shoes."

Eric opened his mouth to say something but Kat immediately cut him off, "No, Eric. You're in the other half." But I have to say that the smile she threw him made me think maybe that wasn't true.

While they all sat there digesting that, Kat gave me a tug that almost spilled my books again. Before I knew what was happening, I found myself pushed into a chair at Kat's table which was full of girls whose names and faces I'd known for years. But I'd never spoken more than a few words to any of them. They were all looking from me to Kat and back again.

"You guys all know Joss, right?"

There were another few awkward moments as the girls muttered and nodded. Then they sort of shrugged and turned back to each other and whatever they'd been talking about before. Backs on either end of the circle turned away from Kat and me, leaving us relatively alone.

"You know that was stupid, right?" I said in a low voice. "Trust me, you do not want to get on Marco's bad side."

"Well hey, you're welcome."

"Yeah, thanks. I'm sure Marco will totally lay off now that you diffused that situation so brilliantly."

"Wow. I've been wondering if you're really the ice bitch everyone says you are."

"Yeah, well, now you know." I started to get up, but Kat put a hand on my arm.

"I'm not sure I do..."

Two of the girls switched seats and Heather pulled her chair up alongside Kat's. Heather was petite and adorable, and just needed a few feathers and fringes to make her look like a Native American princess figurine in a gift shop. I wondered again why I was still there.

"So what was that about? Marco being Marco?"

"Yeah, he seems especially fond of Joss, here."

Heather made a sound in the back of her throat. "I hate that guy."

She looked across at me, an intense look that made me feel like she was seeing too much. I dropped my eyes. "Yeah, me too."

Kat's next remark about Marco's attitude, anatomy, and possible parentage made Heather laugh out loud and even I had to smile.

On possibly the worst day ever, Jocelyn Marshall was sitting in the cafeteria talking to two other girls.

Smiling.

And violations of the Laws of the Universe were just getting started.

CHAPTER 3

Joss

"But Jo-oss, it's too hard. You do it."

"I know I didn't just hear you ask your sister to do your homework, Jilly-bug." Dad came out of the back room, pulling his coat on, and saved me from second grade math homework.

"Um, no way, Daddy!"

"Good. Now honey, are you sure you'll be ok with the Bug?"

"Sure, Dad, it's fine. Don't worry about it."

Dad was going to the range like he always did for the weekly target-shooting match. It was his guy night out, and he'd been doing it for as long as I can remember. Mom, Jill, and I used to watch the store on those nights, but, starting this year, I'd been running the store and closing up by myself. Mostly my parents had been pretty cool about it. A little nervous, maybe, but cool. I'd been working in the store like forever, so no big. But Mom had to go visit her sister out of town that week, so I had Jill and the store. It wasn't any big deal to *me*, but you know dads, right?

Plus there was the thing with Krista. He'd be wigged out about that. I knew he knew. He knew I knew. But we weren't going to talk about it.

"Maybe I should stay."

"Go!" we both ordered.

So Dad gave Jill a smacking kiss on the cheek and walked around the counter to stand in front of me. He grabbed both my hands and looked hard into my face.

19

Dad could change—just like that. One minute he was a normal dad, attentive parent, responsible business owner. The next…

"You're right. We have to keep things normal now. The last thing we want to do is draw attention to ourselves." His voice was low and intense, and his eyes darted to all points around the room and back to mine. Away again. "If you see anything, *anything* suspicious, you know what to do. Under the counter, shotgun. Handgun's under the register. Emergency locks?"

"Panic button in the cabinet locks the door. Exit through the stockroom. Shoot anyone who doesn't follow instructions. Passage behind the boxes in the bathroom leads out to stockroom next door with roof access. Follow planned route across to the next building, down the fire escape to the alleyway. Use untraceable cell phone to contact you to meet us at the rendezvous point."

"And how are you going to contact me with the cell phone if you don't remember to pick up the G.O.O.D. pack?"

G.O.O.D. stands for Get Out Of Dodge. It's important—I really can't stress this enough—it's really important not to roll your eyes at Dad when he goes into commando mode.

"Sorry sir. Secure G.O.O.D. pack from hook next to delivery door before proceeding to bathroom, as pack contains contact phone, provisions, medical supplies, extra ammo, and tear gas which may be necessary in an escape situation."

"Good girl, Joss." And just like that, he started to fade back into normal dad mode. "I did all the checks this morning. You're good to go."

"We're not going to need it, Dad. Everything's fine. Go shoot stuff, 'k?"

"Yeah. Yeah. It's all fine. You're out of here by nine, bed by ten, got it?"

"Yeah, Dad."

Dad gave me a peck on the forehead and walked out of the store without looking back. I knew he was thinking about who might be watching. I took a deep breath and let it out as the tension level immediately dropped back to normal range.

And spiked again when I turned around and Jilly handed me the hugest, pinkest, most beautiful rose anyone has ever seen.

"Do my math, pleeeeeeezzzzz?"

"Jilly! Jesus H. Christ on a Crutch, get rid of that thing right now!"

"Don't you like it? I snagged the leaf from Mrs. O'Neill's yard on the way home from school today."

And then used her Talent to grow that incredible blossom from it, in the palm of her hand. No wonder Dad was a basket case.

"Go to the bathroom and flush it down the toilet. Right. Now."

Jill's face screwed up and her eyes got really bright.

"I love it, ok? It's great. It's the most beautiful thing I've ever seen. And you know we can't keep it. So go get rid of it and when you get back, your homework will magically be done."

"Really?"

"Go!"

Jill slid off her stool and ran off toward the stockroom. I made a mental note to myself to check the place for petals so Dad wouldn't have an embolism.

And you'd think the Universe would have the decency to call it a day by that point, let me relax, feather dust the holster and accessories display, maybe find a better arrangement for the new rifle cases Dad had just leaned up against the wall near the boot "department"… But nooooooo.

Because no sooner had the stockroom door started its backswing, than the sensor on the door that tells us a customer just walked in made its incredibly loud buzz. I just about had a heart attack, thinking it was Dad coming back in to use the bathroom before driving out to the range. But no, even that would have been too much karmic kindness to hope for.

Nope, I jumped up and spun around, with what I'm sure was an oh-so-attractive deer in the headlights look on my face, and my eyes smacked right into Dylan's baby blues as he sauntered into the store.

Gene's Army Navy has all kinds of customers. Even though downtown is having a hard time, and a lot of the stores in the once thriving pedestrian mall—once, like meaning back in the 20's I think—have closed up and moved to the strip malls on the roads out from town, we do ok. I think this is partially due to our wide selection of merchandise. We're not just military surplus, you know. Although we don't sell any firearms because Dad doesn't want to deal with the paperwork for that and get on anybody's "radar."

Plus it helps to be almost right across the bricks from Vinyl Salvation, a pretty cool music store. It used to be a Record World, but it got better. There's a decent thrift shop, with the oh-so-original name Second-Hand Rose, a few doors down from us. And a movie theater—ok, it only has one screen and shows a lot of independent films, but some of them aren't bad—and an ice cream parlor called Sweet Blondies on the corner. Plus there's Pizza Pit.

So we get some kids coming in here sometimes, but thankfully more college kids than kids from my school. We don't have the shoplifting problems that the other stores have because cops shop here sometimes and people think they're friends with my dad, because he sucks up to them and gives them discounts. Then he spends twenty minutes muttering about them as soon as they leave.

So not like Dylan's never been in the store before. He usually just looks around. One time he bought boots. Nice boots, too. My mom waited on him. I remembered I had to count some stuff in the stockroom. And no, that's not hiding. That's being a responsible employee. But now that I had the store to myself on Thursdays, I actually had to stay on the floor and deal.

I expected Dylan to wander the store, but he was coming right at me. Well sure, I thought, 'cause I was standing right behind the glass display case where we kept the knives, and that's one of the things guys like to look at. So I moved aside to, you know, give him some space. His eyes followed me, and his course changed, just that fraction to let me know he was coming toward me, not the knife display.

I hate it when I do the girl thing, even in my head, you know? *Oh my God, he's going to talk to me. Please don't let him talk to me. I'm totally going to curl up and die if he doesn't talk to me.* Ugh.

"Hey."

Hey, Dylan, 'sup?

Hi, welcome to Gene's Army Navy, how can I help you?

Hi, Dylan, how's it goin'?

Hey yourself.

What are you doing here?

"Hey," I replied.

"Um, how's it goin'?"

"S'ok Thursdays are kinda quiet, usually."

He nodded, like he knew. "So...you here alone?"

*Why, are you planning to—*Flippant and highly inappropriate thought crushed beneath my boot before it could make me blush or worse! come out of my mouth. *Be cool.* "Uh-huh."

"Cool." He glanced over at the knife case. See, it was the knives. Did I want him to ask to see one, or was the risk of using it to put myself out of my misery too great at this point? "I wanted to—"

The security buzz blasted from the door again, and we both jumped away from each other. I didn't know what *his* deal was.

"Hi, Mr. Jensen. I thought you'd be at the range tonight."

"No such luck, Jocelyn; couldn't get there tonight. But I was in the neighborhood on my way home and thought I'd check to see if my order came in. It was—"

"The speed-loader pouches. Yeah, they came in the mail little while ago. They're still back in the office. I'll go get 'em."

"Thanks, sweetie."

And maybe, I thought, *Dylan will wander off while I'm back there and find someone else to pick on.* I mean, clearly I had a thing for him, but I marked that down to typical teen female hormonal bad judgment and tried to ignore it as best I could. I'd never really seen him treat anyone the way Marco did, but I felt there was a reasonable guilt-by-association factor involved.

"Jilly, what are you doing?!" She had pulled a chair from the office into the bathroom and there was a tin of grease paint involved.

She jumped down from the chair and ran at me with a war cry. I just stood there, glaring.

"Rawr! I'm a warrior princess! Fear me!"

"Trust me, I do. How many times—"

"I'm going to go scare the customers!"

"I'd rather you—" But I was talking to a swinging door. *Screw it.*

It took me a few minutes to get Mr. Jensen's order because it wasn't even unpacked, the invoices had to be checked against the order, I had to get the special order book and sign off on that form, etc. There's a lot of papers involved, and Dad can be really anal about it.

When I finally got back out on the floor, Mr. Jensen was looking at the belts on the other side of the store, and Dylan and Jilly had their heads together over something on the counter. *No good can come of this*, I thought. The order was paid, so I thanked my customer and wished him a good night. But he hesitated.

"Are you sure you're ok alone?"

"Sure. I manage the store by myself all time."

"I know, it's just…"

I realized he was looking at Dylan. Which made me look at Dylan. And yeah, the boots, leather jacket, that long, somewhat shaggy hair, the shoulders out to here…and there was something about Dylan's quiet, I-could-give-a-shit attitude. While to me these traits added up to a hopeless and ridiculous crush for as long as I could remember, I could kind of see how someone like Mr. Jensen might be concerned. I thought it was sweet. But while we were watching, Jill brought Dylan one of Dad's cleaning rags from under the counter and he used it to wipe the worst of the greasepaint off her hands. *Awwwww.* If a talking gorilla was the next customer through the door, I wouldn't have been surprised at that point.

But anyway, the gesture seemed to reassure Mr. Jensen, so we exchanged pleasantries and he went on his way.

Back at the checkout, Dylan had Jill's pencil and was leaning over her math homework. They were both gonna get it now.

"So look, what I'm saying is, you don't have to have the whole times tables memorized right now to do this stuff. Because you can count really fast, right?"

"1-2-3-4-5-6-7-8-9-10-11-12—"

"Ok, ok. So look here, you've got six times four equals…"

"I don't knooooowwwww," she whined.

"You don't have to *know*. You make some dots—six dots, four times. Like four dice." He did it really fast on the margin of the paper. "Then you count them up. Here, you count. Really fast."

Jill took the pencil and bounced it over the dots. "Twenty-three!"

"Are you sure? Better check."

"Oh, twenty-four."

"That's right! Six times four is twenty-four. So write that down and erase the dots."

She did, and they went on to the next one, which Jill did.

"I don't think she's supposed to do that. I think they're supposed to memorize them."

They both looked at me like I was some kind of narc.

"She will. Eventually. Meanwhile, whatever gets you through math class, right Warrior Princess?"

"Right! I'm gonna get this done 'cause then I can play with my Barbies. You wanna stay and play Barbies when I get done?"

"Um…I'll stay for a while, but I'll probably have to go before Barbie time. Sorry."

"Man, that's tough," I said. "Maybe some other time."

Dylan narrowed his eyes at me, but he was smiling. Then it faded. "Hey, I wanted to talk to you about what happened in the cafeteria today."

I felt myself go stiff. Dylan's nice to my sister and finally proves he's a human. Great. But he was the last person with whom I wanted to discuss my latest school-related trauma. So I went into defense mode. "You want to know if it's true? Why, you got a sister?"

"Look, Marco's an ass. No one disputes this; I've just been around him so long that I'm used to it. I mean, he's also been a dick forever, so I guess I never expect him to grow up and behave like a person."

"If you came in here to apologize for Marco—"

"I came to apologize for me. I should have said something."

Well, that was unexpected. "Like what?"

"Like, I don't know. 'Shut the hell up, asshole,' probably." Then he grimaced. "Eyes on your homework, kid, and keep your ears shut." To me he said, "Sorry," in a stage whisper.

"I'm sure she's heard worse. And if it's that easy, don't worry about it. I'll say it myself next time." Nothing's ever that easy, but I did not want Dylan to pity me because Marco picked on me. That was not the kind of attention I wanted.

No attention was what I wanted, I had to remind myself.

"I just wanted you to know—"

The security buzzer went off again, and we all looked over to see Marco striding in. *Next customer, talking gorilla. How about that?* His eyes scanned the store and when he found Dylan, standing with us at the check out, he seemed surprised and kinda pissed off.

"Hey, I thought we were meeting up at the record store. What're you doin' in here?"

"I'll be over in a few minutes."

"Come over now. That hot chick from the college is workin' tonight."

"I'll be over in a few. Go ahead."

"Why, you buyin' something?"

27

"No, I'm talking to Joss."

"Why?" he asked, like he'd rather shovel horse dung than talk to me, a feeling which was entirely mutual. "Look, Joss, you can come too. But I don't think she's quite your type. Or, wait, you'd be the butch, right?"

"Shut the hell up, asshole," was about all I could think to say.

"You should come. Maybe she'd be into you. I think I'd like to see that."

"All right, that's it. We're leaving." Dylan came around the counter and grabbed Marco by the back of the neck. It wasn't a power play. Dylan's a big guy and he's taller, but Marco's big too, stocky. I was pretty sure he could have broken Dylan's hold easily, if he'd wanted to. Instead he'd gotten his way and let Dylan guide him to the door. "Goodnight, Joss," Dylan called over his shoulder. "Bye, kid." The door security gave out a long buzz and the door swung shut again.

It was hard to see them past the glass because it was dark outside and so bright inside, but I saw Marco knock Dylan's arm away.

"Do you think he likes me?" Jill asked.

"I think he's too old for you."

There was some intense conversation between them for a few moments, and I saw Dylan give Marco a shove. Not hard enough to throw him off balance, more like just to make a point. I wondered what his point was.

"Do you think Dylan likes you?"

"No."

Marco said something else, got the last word in, and turned to walk across the bricks to Vinyl Salvation.

As always, Dylan followed.

* * *

Dylan

"What was that about?" Marco asked, breaking my hold on his neck with an irritated shrug.

"None of your business." At least, I hoped Marco was going to see it that way. I'd let Marco run his mouth about Joss for too long now, hoping he'd just get over it. So she'd turned him down, so what? I was done keeping quiet while Marco worked out his embarrassment or whatever it was. And as long as I was going that far, I might as well be done keeping quiet about my own interest in Joss. Maybe.

One thing at a time. I had other problems with Marco and I didn't really want to bring the whole Joss thing into the middle of it. Then Marco's eyes narrowed on me, and I knew it was too late.

"You've got a thing for that fag-hag, don't you?"

"Cut that shit out, man." Without thinking about it, I spun on Marco and gave him a shove that pushed him back a step.

I hadn't meant to get physical. When we were little kids we had gotten into a fight over some dumb thing and I'd wound up in the hospital. It really scared both of us, and we promised we were never going to fight again. And we hadn't. An apology was halfway out of my mouth before I bit it back. "I'm getting really tired of all the dyke bullshit, ok? It's getting old."

"Whatever. Just don't say I didn't warn you. Somethin's not right about that chick."

Marco turned and headed for the music store. I followed, thinking now was exactly the wrong time to bring up the other thing, but I'd made up my mind to get it out tonight and didn't want to put it off any longer. Besides, when walking into a store with Marco, who knew what he had in mind, or what would come into his head as soon as he saw something he wanted?

"Marco, wait a minute. There's something we gotta talk about."

"So talk."

"Let's hang out here for a minute."

Marco rested his hand on the metal pull of Vinyl Salvation's plexiglass entry door. "What, you need a mocha latté and a muffin? Spit it out."

"I want out."

That got Marco's attention. He walked away to the corner of the building, settled his back against the bricks, and dug a pack of cigarettes out of his jacket.

"So talk," he snapped when I leaned against the wall beside him.

"That's pretty much it. I don't want to do it anymore."

Marco lit his cigarette, blew out smoke. "Huh."

"It was fun, seeing what we could do, what we could get away with. But we're not kids anymore. Swiping nickel and dime shit was one thing, but—"

"We're not kids anymore. It's time for the big stuff— the good stuff. Come on, what's the big deal? You worried about getting tried as an adult? How're they going to catch us?"

How'd they get Krista? "Look, I just don't want to do it anymore, ok? I don't get my rocks off being a criminal. What you do is your business. Just leave me out of any more of your big plans."

Marco was quiet, staring at the smoke curling from the end of his cigarette. I'd expected him to be angry, maybe to shout at me about how much the group needed me, about how I was letting the guys down because I was chicken-shit scared. Whatever he was going to say to try to force me to continue, just to show that I wasn't dickless. But this quiet meant that Marco was thinking, not just reacting.

I was afraid of my best friend. The knowledge sank in my gut like lead. It was more than how I felt a little sick every time he got pissed off about something, more than the start it gave me every time he would give me a shake or a smack. That's just how guys are around each other. It shouldn't have been a big deal. But it was. I had been on the receiving end of that temper once, and I had seen it doled out on someone else. Even knowing that the someone else deserved it, the power of Marco's rage had stuck with me so hard that it had been coloring my actions ever since.

How long had I known what kind of person Marco was becoming and just ignored it? He'd been my best friend practically my whole life. We'd been so close for so long now, that it was like having a brother you couldn't stand, but you'd beat the shit out of anybody who messed with him. If I went with my conscience and stood my ground, would Marco continue to protect me, or throw me to the wolves?

He clapped me on the shoulder, almost making me jump, and flicked the cigarette butt out onto the bricks. I wondered if he knew the effect that had on me. "Like you said earlier, it's best if we lay low for a while. You're right, and we will. But when the time comes, I need you on this. You know I do. I need you to have my back, same way I've always got yours. Anything for a friend, right? Anyway, we can talk about this later. Now come on. College girl's been waiting for me."

CHAPTER 4

Joss

"…and then Sarah's milk *finally* came in—"

"Mo-om…"

"What?"

"TMI. Geez. Let's just leave out any details regarding feeding and digestion, because I swear, if you start describing its poops, I am so out of here."

"Joss, don't you want to hear about your baby cousin's poops?"

"I'm getting my jacket."

"Fine," Mom said airily, gathering up the baby photos she had spread out on the counter. "No more baby talk."

I felt kind of guilty for cutting her off. But I'd already gotten out of bed early on a Saturday to help out at the store and, on top of that, listened to way more details about childbirth and babies than I cared to. There was a limit to daughterly devotion. "You should try Jill. She likes to talk about poop."

"Good plan. So," Mom glanced at me, "anything interesting happen while I was gone?"

"I'm sure Dad told you."

"He did. You okay, sweetie?"

"Sure. Krista was in some of my classes, but I didn't really know her. I was surprised. I didn't know she could do anything. Guess we'll probably never find out what her Talent was. There doesn't seem to be much gossip going around."

"Your dad doesn't know anything either. He doesn't know how they knew about Krista, and that's what's got him most upset."

"How upset is he?" This was code for: *How close is he to completely freaking out?*

Mom's expression tightened, but she kept a smile on and her voice easy. "I think he's okay. It definitely bothers him that no one seems to know about any incident where Krista might have exposed her secret. He thinks that means someone she knew turned her in, probably someone she trusted."

There was code here too. *This is why your dad doesn't want you to get too close to people. This is why we have to be so careful. I wish it didn't have to be like this, but it's only because we love you.*

The front door buzzed, so I took the opportunity to wander away and straighten up. Business started to pick up, and I was busy for the next few hours, cleaning, restocking, and helping customers.

Just before noon I rang up a purchase, handed over the bag, and thanked the customer. When the man walked away he revealed that Kat had been standing behind him.

"Well hi!" She looked out of place in the Army Navy store with her trendy, colorful outfit and bouncy hair.

"Hey. What's up?"

"Do you get a lunch break? I was thinking we could hang out."

"You…were?" Was the store ground zero for random acts of social this week, or was it just more of me as a plaything for the Random Amusements of the Universe?

"Is this your mom? Hi, I'm Kat Dawson." She turned to Mom and stuck out her hand over the counter.

"Joan Marshall. It's nice to meet you, Kat. I guess you know Joss from school?"

"She hasn't mentioned me. She doesn't talk much, does she?"

Mom smiled. "No, I guess she doesn't."

"Well, I talk a lot. And as I'm in need of someone to talk at today, I came to take Joss out to lunch."

"Oh! Well. That sounds nice." Mom tried unsuccessfully to cover her surprise. "Go ahead, honey, get your jacket."

"Um…shouldn't I stay here with you? It's been kind of busy."

"Um…no," Mom actually mocked me, "you should go out with your friend and have a nice time. Your father and I can handle any midday rush. He should be here any minute." This last was said with a gentle emphasis that meant: *So go while you can and before your dad starts asking questions about your friend.*

As much as I was not interested in Kat's lunch plans, I really didn't want to have Dad give either of us the third degree.

We ended up at the Pizza Pit. No big surprise there. It was close to the shop, and that's where kids—and other people sometimes—go to eat. We got slices because they get those out fast.

"Relax," Kat told me, popping the top on her soda can. "I'm not going to ask you about you—yet. Tell me about Krista."

My soda almost came out my nose. *Direct much?* "Um, I didn't really know Krista."

"That's not a huge surprise. You're not exactly ambassador material. But you do pay attention. You're not right in it, but you're watching. All the time. You think a lot."

I didn't know what to say to that. It freaked me out to know that someone was noticing me. Analyzing me.

"Look, everyone's really worked up about Krista. You can feel it, you know? But no one's *talking* about it. I asked a few questions and people got really weird about it. So I get that we're not supposed to talk about it."

"So why are you trying to talk to me about it?"

She leaned back, sipped from her can, and said in a careless, joking tone, "Because even if you think I'm out of line, or suspicious, or whatever it is people think around here for *wanting* to talk about it, who're you gonna tell?"

"Oh! Niiiice." I couldn't help but crack a smile at that. It was the kind of jab I'd make at myself. It was kind of ok to have her make it instead.

"So come on. I know Krista must have had a Talent. She wasn't the first kid to ever be taken to a State School, but she is the first one I ever met."

"She wasn't the first one from around here, ok? There have been…a bunch."

"What's a bunch?"

"I don't know. Enough so it's a thing here. A thing we don't talk about. Enough so we start to think there must be more. And we wonder if the person sitting next to us is hiding a Talent."

"And there's probably a bunch of Talents around wondering if the person next to them is gonna figure them out and turn them in."

I took a bite of pizza while she was talking, not caring how it burned the roof of my mouth. At least she couldn't read anything from my expression except *Oh my God, cheese burn!* Kat bit into hers too, with more care than I had, and we ate in silence for few minutes. But of course I knew she wasn't finished.

"So these kids who disappear, they never come back?"

"No."

"No letters? Phone calls?"

I wiped my mouth, trying to figure out what to tell her and thinking that Dad was so right about how having friends would just complicate my life, make me constantly have to decide what to say and what not to say.

"A long time ago, there used to be some letters. But they were censored. You know, lots of lines marked through with black marker so you couldn't read them. Then there was this big deal where someone managed to reconstruct what had been censored. I think it was someone with a Talent who did it, but I'm not sure how it happened. It was just a flash in the media—something that came out and was hushed up really fast. Most major news outlets, papers and stuff, didn't run it. It would be hard to track down anything about it now."

"But you heard about it."

"Like you said, I listen a lot."

"Ok, so the reconstructed letter. What did it say?"

I looked around. I didn't know why I was telling her this stuff. I had this feeling like I *wanted* to tell her. It wasn't like I was getting more comfortable with talking to her. But it almost felt like some kind of release to tell her, to talk to someone about this stuff I knew. It was weird, but I liked it. So I was going to keep going.

"It talked about what it was really like at the State Schools. Like prison. It talked about working the kids to improve their Talents, but like hard. Like you can make your players do laps to get them in better shape, or you can make them run until they drop and then kick them until they get up and make them run some more. It was like that. It talked about experiments. Torture. Food and sleep deprivation. Just all kinds of horrible stuff. That sense that everyone has that they do *not* want to go to a State School, despite what the government says about helping Talents? The Koenig Letter—that's what they called it—is part of that. Even if they missed it when it happened, that's what started the rumors flying. That's when NIAC became the Boogeyman."

"Wow, you even remember the name."

I flushed. *Damn.* "Yeah, well, it's just... living here where it's been more common, I guess it's more interesting to me than it is to other people. Plus, I'm good with names. I know a lot of crap."

"Uh huh. Yeah, I guess I can see that. So after the...whatever Letter thing, then no more letters?"

"Right. Supposedly the point of the State Schools is to help kids with Talents control them—so they don't hurt anybody. And at first that's mostly who they took." Part of me was telling myself to shut up, but I was just in it now, wanting to be able to tell someone how wrong it all was. "But that didn't cover the kids who didn't electrocute the cat, or shatter all the windows, or start f-fires—" I took another drink so I could swallow. "But they wanted control over all the kids. So they said that scientists should have access to all the Talents. That's when they made it mandatory for parents to report their kids. But since the 'dangerous' Talent kids never came back, who's going to do that, right? Not a lot of parents did.

"Then, not too long after that, came the R.J. Smith Elementary School Disaster. Allegedly there was one psychic kid who could put thoughts in other people's heads. You'd think he would have made himself the most popular kid in school, but I guess he wasn't really bright. He had some family problems, and other kids made fun of him because of that, so rather than change their minds, he got back at them by screwing with their heads. Scaring the hell out of them. Until some of them started killing in self-defense—against whatever was in their heads—killed each other, a teacher. It was a whole big mess."

"My God."

"Yeah. Total psycho little kid. So there's an example of a Talent you can't really see, and that you wouldn't necessarily *think of* as going to go out of control. Not like toddlers who turn the babysitter into a popsicle. But obviously people can still be hurt by stuff like that, so the government says, that's it, we don't know what the kids can do, what they *will* do. They're just kids, and we need to look out for all of them in a controlled environment. So that's when the scare campaign really got going and, unlike the Koernig thing, the government was all over publicizing the Smith School Disaster. They made it everyone's civic duty to turn in Talents. So now it wasn't just parents, it was teachers, day care workers, neighbors, anyone who saw a kid use a Talent should report it. Because if something awful happens, it's gonna be on your head."

"I never heard that before. But then, my parents aren't really into talking about national events and politics and stuff. We hardly ever even watch the news."

"It was a long time ago. Like when we were really little, I guess. I bet if you ask your parents, they'll remember the school thing."

"Yeah, maybe." She gave me that look again, that sort of assessing look that made me nervous. "So, you really can talk when you get into it. It's a different you. You're all…animated."

Yeah, great, thanks. "I should go. Saturday's busy sometimes. My parents might be swamped." I pushed my chair back.

"Ok. Look, Joss, thanks for telling me this stuff. I'm sorry I'm so pushy. I get that it makes you uncomfortable."

"No big deal."

"I'm sorry for that crack earlier about who're you gonna tell."

I shrugged. "It's true enough. Don't worry about it."

"Yeah, but, I was kind of hoping that we could be friends."

I opened my mouth to ask her why, but then shut it again. That's what she expected me to say; that was how she was going to keep me here, talking to her. And who knows what I'd say if I did that.

"I should go. Thanks for lunch."

CHAPTER 5

Joss

There were footsteps on the stairs, heavy and quick, jogging up, then down again.

False alarm.

I went back to my book. I was sitting on the uppermost landing of the stairwell at the end of the science wing. Fairview High was a Frankenstein's Monster of a building, with all kinds of additions grafted onto the original part of the school. It was a desperate attempt to keep up with the times, without actually tearing it apart and starting over. My spot, the one I had found in the first months of my freshman year, was in the older part. The stairwell was one of those dark, steep, wrap-around deals, far enough away from everything else that it didn't get much traffic. Most kids stuck to the more central stairs.

This landing I was perched on was the end of a road to nowhere. The stairs continued up, past the second floor, for no apparent reason. I think maybe they meant to put in a roof access door or something like that, but it didn't happen. So there was no reason for anyone to come up this far. Plus, because of the way the stairs were all but stacked on top of one another, you really couldn't see from one landing up to the next. Although you could see down if you leaned forward and looked through the railing. All in all, it made it a really great place to hide and get a little peace in the chaos of Hell on Earth. Which I really needed, regularly. That's why it was My Spot.

I wasn't supposed to be in that part of the school so early in the morning. No one was. But it was one of those days when the pouring rain was so bad that they couldn't make everyone stay outside until the first bell, so they had to let them all into the lobby and the gym. School, after all, is a place of learning, and you can't just have students roaming its halls. Who knows what might happen? But, even when they open up the gym, it gets really crowded and there are kids, like me, who always manage to escape the corral. Even if it means manipulating a locked gate or two along the way.

I heard the footsteps again, slower this time, and a few more of them. My heartbeat picked up as I shoved the novel back in my bag and reached for the Chem text. After all, maybe the appearance of scholarly duty would soften the heart of an over-zealous hall monitor and save me from detention.

But since when did hall monitors travel in packs?

Marco rounded the corner and stopped as soon as he saw me. He was clearly surprised. In the next moment, when he started up the steps toward me, and that predatory smile started to spread across his face, you could tell he was pleased in his evil way.

"Hey, Joss…You know…you're not supposed to be here."

I suck at this, I really do. There must be some way, some right thing to say to diffuse this and make him go away. But I didn't know what it was. During the recent cafeteria incident I had tried not saying anything, but that hadn't worked. So this time I went for mild sarcasm.

"Huh. You don't say?"

Marco sneered at me and continued up the steps, made a show of easing himself slowly down to sit beside me. And of course, since I was leaning against the railing and there were only four whole feet of floor beside me, he had to sit right up against me. *This is what crawling skin feels like, when your whole skin wants to crawl away from something noxious, whether the rest of you is coming along or not.* I wasn't about to give him the satisfaction. He'd probably make himself comfortable and bug me until the bell. I could deal that long without shoving him down the stairs. Probably.

Jeff came up next, pulling some girl behind him. Some girl who seemed reluctant to follow. He pulled her up onto the landing and pushed her back into the corner. Not a shove, not violent, but it was a push. I felt a flare of something, rage or human decency, probably some combination of the two. But I breathed in and beat it down. Whatever this was, it was not my business. Still, it seemed not good, and I was starting to feel uneasy about more than just Marco occupying my personal space.

In that moment, before Jeff blocked her from my view, she looked up.

I jumped back on instinct, right into Marco who used the opportunity to throw his arm around my shoulders. I don't think Trina saw me. She might have seen a flash of someone, assumed Marco was watching them. Leaning away from Marco again I took a chance, leaned toward the railing again and peeked through the bars.

Jeff had Trina completely caged, almost completely hidden by his tall body. I could see part of the side of her, one leg, covered in black tights below her skirt, bent at the knee, her whole body sort of trying to turn protectively away from him. His hand skimmed up the sleeve of her light jacket, caught the strap of her bag that she wore over one shoulder, and pulled it off, dropping it to the ground beside them. The move tugged her jacket and sweater out of place to bare her shoulder. She didn't move to fix her clothes, but she didn't look at him either.

Beside me, as my stomach clenched, Marco leaned into my ear. "Do you like to watch?"

I wanted to ask him what was going on, but I was afraid to turn my face toward his, afraid and disgusted by the intimacy of our conversation as well as the scene below us. I was afraid to ask because I was afraid to know. Because knowing for sure that something was wrong would morally obligate me to act to stop it, wouldn't it?

And I couldn't do that.

Jeff leaned in and was saying something to Trina. Her face was turned away, toward the corner, but I could see her body language, see her cringe. Unconsciously I mimicked her movement. That caused Marco to chuckle softly. He lifted his arm from around my shoulders, but before I could be relieved, he quickly shifted his position, sliding up and back, getting one leg on the other side of me. He wrapped his arms around my waist and hauled me back, snug against him, dropping his chin on my shoulder so that we were both looking over the railing.

Somehow I had let that happen. That disgusting pig had his whole body wrapped around mine and I just sat there and took it. I didn't shriek, throw him off, pummel him senseless—all the kinds of reactions that I would never allow myself because they would draw too much attention. Maybe that doesn't make a lot of sense, but I'd spent my whole life learning to tread as lightly as I could, always concerned about not making anyone notice me. If I started yelling my head off and teachers came rushing to my aid, I'd have to explain why I was up here, illegally, in the first place. They'd remember me. I'd be on their radar. Other kids might see or hear, start wondering aloud why I was up here, alone with Marco. Start talking about me, noticing me. I couldn't have that. I had to stay cool.

Cool and completely grossed out.

I forced myself to be calm. *Being this disgusted isn't fatal,* I thought. *Probably.* I could just wait it out, until Marco was done messing with me. Let him lose interest as usual and be on his way. I was in no real danger, after all. We were in school, right? What was really going to happen? If he tried anything, I could knock him down the stairs. Or there were other things I could do. My dad might want me to pretend to be normal around other people, but at home he had made me practice, build up my control so I was ready for all kinds of scenarios.

Below us, Jeff lowered his mouth to Trina's shoulder. My stomach rolled. I knew *my* reasons for not screaming bloody murder, but what were hers? Why the hell didn't she knee him in the balls or something? Her hand came up between them, ineffectually pushing at his chest. He caught it and brought it up behind her back, forcing her to arch into him. I felt queasy.

Inside, my conscience was screaming at me to do something, but the part of my mind that was always in control, that monitored every single step I took to make sure it wouldn't cause anyone to look my way? It was stronger, louder, telling me that if we could just hold out a few more moments, surely this would stop. So some gross guy was pawing at her. She'd live, right? My eyes were hot, and I was getting afraid that tears were actually going to come out of them. My heart pounded as I tried to think ahead, tried to bargain with myself.

Ok, it's ok. Just stay calm. This is under control. It's not like she can't help herself. And if it seems like she really can't, then you still can, right? If it goes too far, you can still do something. Like knock Jeff's head into the wall, push him back, watch him bounce down the stairs. Just hang on and don't do anything you'll regret.

But just how far was too far? Jeff's leg slid between Trina's. I didn't know where his other hand was—I didn't want to know. His mouth was on hers and she was squirming against him, but he had her pinned, completely under his control. I could…What could I do? Send that bag of books into his head? Of course not. Way too obvious. Send a punch of air to hit the backs of his knees? Tricky from this far away, but yeah, maybe that. Maybe a blow to his kidney to throw him off enough for her to get loose? Would she even run off if I set her free?

And would Marco be able to figure out that I had done it?

I barely heard the quick, light footsteps on the stairs, but I heard them, and so did Marco whose body went tense. Jeff was oblivious.

"Oh! Um, sorry! I'll just…" the girl's voice sounded familiar and trailed off when Jeff's head spun around to see who it was.

"What do you want?" he snarled. Now that he had moved, I could see Trina's swollen mouth, smeared lipstick, and the tracks of tears on her cheeks. My own eyes—there was just no way I was gonna cry. No way. Why the hell was she letting this happen to her?

Why was I?

"Hey, Trina. You ok?" I heard the footsteps again, and brown curls came into view.

It was Kat.

"Get lost." Jeff shifted to block Trina in again.

"What the hell's going on here? Trina, come with me."

"She's fine, and I told you to get lost."

I hadn't thought my heart could pound any harder, but my whole head was pulsing with blood and tension. I didn't know Kat very well, but she didn't seem like the type to just turn around and leave, and I knew Jeff was a hot-head. Yesterday I probably wouldn't have thought he'd hit a girl, but that was yesterday. I risked a glance at Marco, who was riveted…and smiling.

Jeff turned to Kat and took a step toward her, well into her personal space. Kat didn't back down, but it was obvious by the way she leaned away as she looked up at him that she was uncomfortable.

Behind Jeff, I could barely hear Trina saying, "Kat, just go."

"Yeah, this is *private*." Jeff gave her a shove that was more like a hard punch to the shoulder, and made her stumble sideways toward the stairs.

She grabbed him to steady herself, but then hung on to his arm. He started to shake her off, but she just latched on to the front of his jacket.

"Jeff," she said firmly, staring into his eyes. "Go away."

He jerked slightly, as though she'd dealt him a slap that didn't so much hurt as surprise him. Then, in the next moment he stumbled back, out of her grip, his hands coming up to his face.

"What the hell? What did you do, you bitch?" His hands moved over his face, seeking some kind of injury or something. "What did you do??" He pressed his back to the wall, his eyes wide with terror and darting around everywhere. He groped for the railing.

"You'll be fine if you get out of here before you really piss me off." Kat's voice was deadly.

Jeff was swiping at his eyes with the back of one hand, the other on the handrail. He moved quickly down the steps, missing some, half falling, catching himself and continuing down. Totally panicked.

I realized that both Marco and I were standing and leaning over the railing, watching his progress, stunned by what we had seen. Marco snapped into action, forgetting about me and racing down the stairs. I followed.

"What the hell did you do to him?" Marco snarled, grabbing Kat's arm and jerking her around to face him.

"You...probably don't want to do that," I said. Suddenly I was shocked that I had even followed him, let alone opened my mouth to get involved. I immediately wished I could disappear. But it worked. Marco let go of Kat like she was made of fire.

Kat looked at me, and I didn't like what I saw on her face. I could feel my cheeks getting red and my stomach sinking, wondering what she was thinking about me just then. About what I was doing up there with Marco. Watching.

"I didn't do anything to your friend. I don't know why he got all freaked out. Go see for yourself; he's probably fine."

Marco shoved past her and down the stairs after Jeff. Kat shot me another glare and turned to Trina, reaching out.

"You okay? Come on, let's—"

Trina jerked back against the wall, away from Kat's touch. "You stay the hell away from me. What the hell *are* you?" She flashed a glance at me, a glance that spoke eloquently of shared memory, perception—however false—and loathing. I wanted to open my mouth, to deny what I knew she was thinking, but I didn't. I felt myself take a step back from the force of her glare, which she turned back on Kat. "Why don't you just mind your own damned business? I want you to stay away from me, you freak. Clear?"

"Crystal." From the set of Kat's jaw, I knew she was dying to lash out at Trina, but she held it in. I thought that was really decent of her.

Trina hurried down the steps away from us, clutching her bag across her chest with one arm, the handrail with her free hand. She was obviously really shaky, but determined to get away from the scene, from Kat, from me. She made the second floor landing safely and hurried out of our sight.

Kat turned to me. Or, I should say, *on* me. "Was that fun for you?"

"Um, *no*," I said with as much bitch as I could put into it. Because I didn't really know what else to say. I knew how it looked.

In my head I saw the accusing way Trina had looked at me. Like she thought I'd waited all these years for payback. Yeah, right. What was the point? Nothing I could do to her would fix what she'd done when we were kids. Nothing was going to make me feel better about it. Ever. And you know, that whole time I was stuck up there with Marco, *none* of that stuff about the fire went through my head. It was just about what Jeff was doing to this other girl, this other girl who maybe could have been me—*maybe*. Not what Jeff was doing to Trina who'd ruined my life and totally deserved what she was getting. No one deserved that.

"Well, I hope you enjoyed the show."

Kat started to leave and I reached out for her arm. Something I *never* do, but I was in a weird place just then. She looked at my hand, looked at my face.

"You probably don't want to do that," she mocked me.

I yanked my hand back, not because I was scared of her, but just because I could hardly believe I had reached out to her in the first place.

"I'm sorry. Look, it's just…You shouldn't have done that. I mean, it's bad enough to get on Marco's bad side, but showing those guys what you can do like that is just stupid."

"Is that what you were doing up there? Staying on Marco's good side?" Kat's voice was dripping with nasty innuendo.

"No!" *And maybe, kinda? In a way? Ugh. I'm subhuman.* "I was already there, ok? I like to hang out there. It's *my* spot."

"I know. I was looking for you."

How would you—? Whatever. "And then Marco came up, and Jeff and Trina were behind him and that whole thing started and he made me sit there and—"

"He made you."

"Well, yeah. I mean, what was I supposed to do?"

"Oh, I don't know, Joss, stick up for her? Say something? Call someone?"

"*She* didn't. Look, I didn't understand what was going on, and it wasn't any of my business. So I stayed out of it. And that's what you should have done because now you're totally on Marco's shit-list, and that is not where you want to be. He'll do nothing but make trouble for you. And now he knows about your…Jesus, Kat. Who knows what he's going to do with that?"

"What are *you* going to do with it?"

"I? What, like you think I'm going to tell someone about this? Who would I even tell?"

She sniffed. "Yeah, I guess." She started down the steps, stopped, and didn't turn to look at me.

"You're not who I thought you were."

CHAPTER 6

Dylan

Eric was telling me something about some car. He was always talking about cars, and even though it was usually interesting stuff, I wasn't listening. I was watching Joss.

Truth be told, I was watching Joss a lot lately. One minute I was like—*to hell with you, Marco, get over yourself.* And the next I went back to thinking that things between Marco and me were bad enough already right now without causing more trouble.

Not like other girls. There's an understatement. It's like there were all the other girly girls with their hair-flipping, laughing at everything you say, talking about the labels of everything they wore… All the other things they did to get attention. And then there was Joss, who wore a bulky field jacket over jeans and t-shirts all year 'round. With combat boots. And who seemed to do whatever she could to be as invisible as possible.

Man, would she be jealous if she knew what I could do. Or not. Maybe she'd be freaked out.

She was talking to Kat, which was unusual. Joss pretty much always left right after the bell, without talking to anyone. But she'd been acting strange—stranger than normal—all day. She was quieter, more withdrawn, more troubled. And yeah, that was Joss…only moreso.

Besides the fact that just her being there and seeking someone out to talk was weird, the way they were talking was weird. They were too close for Joss, who always seemed to need a lot of distance, with their heads bent together, their conversation obviously private and intense. Joss's expression was more than her usual blank mask. She looked like she was asking for something. That glossy dark hair of hers was down, curling around her face. It blew across her cheek and she reached up to tuck it behind her ear.

Damn, even that was hot.

I was turning into a stalker.

Eric nudged me in the ribs. Eric was one of those guys who always seemed to see what was going on, even when you thought you were being cool. He probably knew I wasn't listening to a word he was saying, knew I was watching Joss, and knew I wouldn't want Marco seeing me doing it. Which was cool of him. Marco was finally showing up; he had Rob Grayson with him.

This was not a good sign. Rob didn't hang with us; he was a geek. And I'm not saying that means he wasn't good enough to hang with us. More like he was too smart to want to. We didn't really have much in common, and Rob might as well hang an *I'd Rather Be Playing Chess* sign around his neck. The only time Marco dragged him into our group was when he wanted Rob to do something for him. Something criminal.

Last time, he'd had Rob hack into some computer and place fake orders for some stereo equipment, marked paid, to be delivered to his cousin's house. He and his cousin had sold most of it. I didn't know if Rob had done it for a cut of the money, which he'd gotten, or if it was just 'cause Marco intimidated him.

Marco liked money. And he was enjoying coming up with this kind of stuff and getting away with it. I think, for him, the stereo plot was just a test. A test for Rob. Now Rob was in, whether he liked it or not.

Just like I was.

"All right, listen up. Jeff, you've heard this already, so you're on look-out right now. Look cool, but ignore us and just give us a heads up if someone gets too close."

Jeff nodded, pleased. He liked knowing things first. He actually liked it when Marco told him to do stuff, singled him out. I'd been friends with Jeff almost as long as I'd been friends with Marco, but sometimes I had to wonder about him.

"So what's the deal?" Eric asked.

"We're goin' beer shopping."

"Beer?"

"*Lots* of beer. We're gonna hit FoodsMart."

"A supermarket?" *Not good. Not good.* Lots of security, and way too much temptation for these guys once we were inside. And no way was I doing this. "You can't just boost a few cases from a mini mart anymore?"

"No, I said *a lot* of beer. Kegs, cases, whatever. Party."

"But—"

"I've already got a couple buyers lined up. We're committed to this. And it's not rocket science, Dylan. You and Rob are going in the store while it's still open. You're going to cover Rob and sneak into the storeroom. Find a place to hang tight until closing. Jeff and I have been watching. On weeknights they close up at eleven and everyone is gone before midnight. So you guys are going to wait until midnight. Then you work your way out of the storeroom, back to the front of the store. You'll be doing your thing and staying between Rob and cameras. There's an Employees Only door near the bathrooms, across from the checkouts. The lock's electronic and shouldn't be any problem for Rob, here." He slung his arm around Rob's shoulders, a move that looked more like imprisonment than friendship. Rob continued to watch his own feet.

"Behind the door are the steps that go up to the office. I know someone who used to work there, and she says there are no cameras beyond the door and all the locks are electronic."

"Damn, Marco, how many people know about this?"

"Don't worry about it. Once you're upstairs, you just shut down the cameras and alarms. Get the keys to unlock the back door, the one where the employees hang out and smoke. Come back and let us in.

"Eric, I'm gonna need you to boost us a delivery truck. Nothing too flashy, something that would be out at night, but not something anyone's gonna miss either. You'll need to start looking around for that."

"Right."

"Once we've got what we came for, Eric, Jeff, and I are leaving in the truck. But you guys need to get back to the office. I'll take care of breaking the camera over the back door while we're in there. You guys turn all the cameras and alarms back on—except you've gotta disable the sensor on that back door. If you can't do it, you're gonna have to sleep there and leave in the morning."

"I can do it," Rob mumbled.

"Right. So Dylan, you cover Rob, just like before, on the way out. You can leave the keys in the door like someone forgot them, or you can pitch 'em in a dumpster somewhere. Whatever. Meet us back at the shack when you're done."

"I don't know, Marco…" I started, getting ready to argue.

"You don't have to know. That's my job."

"It's one thing to cover Rob hiding out in the store room, in case anybody sees us. Standing still, that's no big deal. But moving around like that? Multiple cameras? I just don't know."

"But you're gonna find out. You're gonna need to spend some time in the store, getting the lay of the land. You're gonna get back into the storeroom and watch what people go for, and where they don't go. Find the best place for you and Rob to chill out until closing. And you're probably gonna do a dry run of the offices, during business hours, before we do this thing."

"What the fuck, Marco? I'm not breaking into any office during business hours. Have you lost your mind?"

Marco gave me a hard glare. "You guys are gonna want to get into that office before we do this so Rob can access the cameras and get downloads from all the feeds. So you'll be able to find the blind-spots—or the blindest spots. You'll want to know where you're going when we do the job, right? You're also gonna log some practice time, you and Rob, moving together, and the rest of us are going to watch to see how good a job you do keeping him covered."

"This is way too complicated. And for beer? Come on, Marco. Give me a break. You want beer, let's hit Casey's. One camera, one employee…"

"This is what we're doing, Dylan, and I'm getting tired of your bullshit whining."

"Seriously, grow some balls, man," Jeff put in, still casually scanning the grounds.

"This isn't about balls, it's about brains," I told Jeff. "And if you had any at all—but then what do you have to do but go in the back and put some beer in a truck? Or is Jeff just gonna be the lookout?"

It was dumb to antagonize them, but damn. I saw Marco look at me hard before Jeff shoved me into Eric. Then he was all up in my face, with Eric trying to get between us.

"Knock it off." Marco grabbed Jeff with one hand and yanked him off me. Jeff worked his shoulder, trying to be casual, but I knew that had to hurt. "And you too," he said to me. "You wanna know more about the plan, you ask me later. But we're doing this, and that's the end of it."

Marco took a step back and looked around, scanning the grounds to see if anyone was taking too much notice of us or the scuffle. Then he smiled, and was looking off in the direction where Joss and Kat were sitting on a rock wall near the street.

"Now, if you'll excuse me, I see some ladies who need my attention."

I pushed away from the wall, ready to follow him, but Eric grabbed my arm. I looked at him. He shook his head.

I got the message.

Not the time to mess with him.

I knew he was right. And I hated it.

* * *

Joss

"It wasn't how it looked."

"Really? 'cause it looked like you and Marco—who I *thought* you didn't like—were getting all cozy up there in the stairwell, that you knew Jeff was messing with that girl and you did absolutely nothing about it. Do you really have something against Trina? Did you think it was funny, or you just didn't care?"

I opened my mouth and closed it again. I didn't even know which of those to deal with first. I thought about the look Trina gave me before she left, the one that said she thought I'd enjoyed watching Jeff mess with her because I hated her.

"Look, I'm sorry I didn't do anything and you had to get involved, ok? I was having some of my own problems at the time, and if Trina didn't make any effort to help herself, what was I supposed to do?"

"She was scared."

"So was I!"

Kat gave me her piercingly assessing look again. I'd never thought of myself as prone to blurting out stupid things like that, but I wasn't used to talking a whole lot. I realized I had people avoidance almost down to an art form. I never had to have personal conversations unless it was deflecting my parents, which didn't count.

"Anyway," I said, trying to redirect, "I'm sorry for what I said to you after. It was cool, what you did—whatever it was. You stand up, and that's cool." How many times was I going to say 'cool'? "It's just I've been on Marco's bad side for a while now and I know it's a lousy place to be. You've pissed him off twice in two weeks."

"Which gives me a warm, fuzzy feeling inside."

"See? This is what I'm saying. You're not taking me seriously."

"Why Joss, it almost seems like you care."

What was I supposed to say to that? She was teasing me, but it was friendly. I didn't know how to deal with that. So I decided it was time to shut up.

"I made him blind."

"Beg pardon?"

"When I grabbed onto Jeff, I concentrated on how pissed off I was and he went blind. Just temporarily. Like maybe a minute or two."

What the Hell was wrong with this girl? "Why did you tell me that? That's exactly what I'm talking about. It's like nothing I said to you on Saturday sunk in at all. It's bad enough you've got a Talent, but you're in Fairview now. I told you we've got way more than other places and it's always on people's minds. I've seen way too many kids disappear because they were careless, because they trusted the wrong people. So don't be stupid."

"Yep," she grinned, "you like me. We're going to be really good friends."

"That's great," I said, getting up from the stone wall we were sitting on, "I always like it better when the school day ends with a threat."

"Hey, you're funny!"

"Of course she is." I cringed the moment before Marco's arm landed across my shoulders. "That's our Joss. It's cool that I find you two together, because that means Joss gets to see more of this unfolding drama."

I groaned inwardly. When Marco started waxing like that, it meant he had been thinking too much.

"What I've been thinking," he continued, as though he could hear my thoughts, "is that I am now in possession of valuable information. And before you both insult me by playing dumb, I'll spell it out: Kat, here, has a Talent. She blinded Jeff when she grabbed him this morning." Marco snickered. "You really scared the shit out him—for the whole two minutes it lasted. He's *really* pissed at you, by the way. He was ready to tell anyone who'd listen until someone came to haul your ass off to State School."

"Marco, I don't even know what you're talking about."

"See, that's what I mean about the playing dumb and insulting. But that's ok, because you're cute when you're helplessly screwed. So, like I was saying, Jeff's ready to blab your secret all over town, but don't worry, because I stopped him from doing that."

I wanted to say *Gee, that's nice,* or something snarky, but I couldn't bring myself to open my mouth.

"And that's really nice of me, right? I mean, standing between you and Jeff like that—well, really, between you and the State School and who knows what they do there. Seems like that ought to be worth something."

"All this, assuming I had a clue what you're talking about, which I don't."

"See, I'm betting that it doesn't matter if you admit to what you did or not. Jeff knows you did. I saw you do it. So what you've got to ask yourself is: will anyone believe us if we tell? Now…you might want to tell yourself that you can toss your hair and flash a smile and talk your way out of—whatever. But really, we're talking about two witnesses vs. a suspected Talent who *allegedly* used her ability *against* another person. I'm thinkin' that plan's not going to work too well for you.

"So here's what I'm offering: my silence, and Jeff's silence, guaranteed, your freedom and secrecy secure, for the low, low price of just $500."

"You've got to be kidding me."

"I'm. So. Not." Marco was dead serious now. "You think about it. You get the money together. You've got two weeks. Now bye-bye, see ya, wouldn't wanna be ya!" He ruffled my hair and pushed at my head as he walked away, enough to make me take a step to keep my balance.

"Gawd, what an idiot," Kat said, disgusted.

"What are you going to do?"

"Nothing."

I swear I wanted to grab her and shake. Hard. "What do you mean, *nothing*?"

"I'm not paying that bastard so he can go enrich the porn industry, or whatever. Screw that. And screw him."

"Kat…"

"I don't know, Joss. I need to think about this. But I'm not paying him."

Suddenly, I could tell that she was shaken. I decided to back off.

"I could help. I've got some money saved."

Kat looked surprised, then smiled, but not as brightly as she usually did. She touched my arm, briefly. "Thanks, Joss. That's really nice. I told you we'd be friends, didn't I?" A horn beeped. "Look, that's my mom. I gotta go."

She got in the car and they drove off, leaving me alone on the sidewalk, thinking about how the last thing I wanted was a friend with a Talent who would get herself hauled off to the nearest State School.

CHAPTER 7

Joss

You realize, of course, that you are a complete idiot.
Well, conscience, I'd say that much is obvious.

Such were my thoughts as I made my way from the safety of my stairwell down to the cafeteria at about half past lunchtime. Truth be told, ever since I'd had to share my space with Marco, all his limbs, and his unfortunate idea of entertainment, I was really soured on what had been my own little corner of Fairview High for the last few years.

Needless to say that the cafeteria was chaos as usual, and yeah, it scared the crap out of me. But at least this time I had a clear objective in my sights, and I was more wary of skirting too close to the muck this time.

Kat was sitting with the same group she had been with the other day: Heather, Maddy, and Elizabeth. Maddy's brother Matt was there too, straddling a backward chair between Maddy and Kat and talking intently to his sister about something. Maddy raised a gloved hand—part of her unique style was to always wear these thin, leather cyclist gloves—and gave Matt the finger with a sneer on her pixie-like features. And that's when they looked up and saw me standing there, rather awkwardly, holding my books in front of me in that way I remembered I shouldn't but couldn't change now.

Not so much a sense of *everybody knows your name and they're always glad you came,* so much as startled bewilderment from everyone at the table. But Matt immediately got up and spun the chair around.

"Want my seat, Joss? I was just leaving."

I felt my face getting hot. "Oh, no, you don't have to—"

"No, really, I'll be contemplating twinnicide if I spend another minute with this brat." He cuffed Maddy on the back of her short, platinum hair. "Take it."

"Um, thanks."

Matt wandered away and I thought, not for the first time, how different they were. Him big, kind of brawny, but with that whole prep-school wannabe thing he had going. Her small and slight, but also edgy, looking like a punk-rock fairy. And really, Matty and Maddy? Naming your daughter Matilda is bad enough, but the naming police ought to come and shoot their parents.

"So, Joss, cool to see you. What brings you to the cafeteria?"

That's a good question, Kat. What the hell was I thinking? I'd been so into talking to her, about what had happened after school the day before, that I hadn't even thought about the fact that I'd never be able to get a private word in this place. *Great.* I casually turned my head to glance around the room and saw several people look quickly away, including Dylan, and made a note-to-self never to do this again.

"Not much, really. I wanted to ask you if I could talk to you—after school—if you're not busy or anything."

"Really?"

"Um, yeah, but it's no big—"

"No! That totally works because I was going to ask *you* to come over to my house today."

I glanced around the table. Maddy was talking quietly to Elizabeth—who I don't think ever talked any other way than quietly. They were a study in opposites with Maddy's rebel looks and Elizabeth's classic shy girl chic. Heather caught my glance, smiled, and moved her chair around the table to get in on their conversation, leaving Kat and me a little more privacy. "Your...house?" I stuttered. You'd think she'd invited me to her family crypt, as freaked out as I was by the invitation.

"Yeah, you know, where I live, with my parents. And I keep my room there too."

"Huh. Interesting."

"So...will you come over?"

"Why?"

Kat made a disgusted noise in the back of her throat. "Because that's where I keep my Great Big Book of Manners by Emily Post and I want to beat you with it."

I was totally confused and just looked at her blankly.

Which got me another disgusted noise and a bonus eye-roll. "Never mind. I wanted to talk to you, too. About some stuff I don't want to talk about here." This last was said with a meaningful look.

"Oh. Well, ok. I guess so."

She flashed that freakishly charming smile at me. I could feel the corners of my own mouth want to turn up. I wondered if it was another Talent or if she was just born with the dose of charisma the Charm Angel forgot to give me. Though I had been heretofore convinced that my lack was a genetic defect inherited from my dad—and not much missed.

"Great! So meet me in front after school—same place I was yesterday, and my mom will pick us up, okay?"

"I...I should probably go home," I hedged. "My mom's expecting me..." The subject of me going to a friend's house instead of walking straight home had never come up before. I wasn't sure how that worked.

"Oh, you can call her from my house. And if it's a problem, my mom will just drive you home. But it won't be, 'cause your mom likes me, and wants you to spend more time with me."

The fact that was probably true made me scowl darkly at her.

"So you'll come, right? Because I really want us to talk."

"Yeah, I'll come." *But only because a chance to talk some sense into you was what I wanted in the first place.*

"Yay!" And then she hugged me.

Geez.

* * *

Joss

There was a lot of pink in Kat's room. Bright pink, bright aqua, bright yellow. You get the idea. All matching white furniture on a wood floor scattered with bright rugs. Thanks to my little sister, I could recognize Hello Kitty and friends when I saw them, but I had no idea who the hunky guys on the walls were. I was really behind on current popular culture.

Kat had me sitting in a giant hot pink and chrome chair that resembled a satellite dish but made me feel sort of like my ass was perched in King Kong's palm. Or possibly it was the collection of stuffed animals on the bed that made me feel threatened.

I had already called my mom from the comfort of the Dawsons' spacious living room. It seemed like practically every room in the house got a dose of her mom's affection for porcelain dolls and figurines. They were all staring at me and creeping me out. But anyway, like Kat had predicted, mom sounded happy about me spending time over here. "Of course it's ok for you go to a friend's house, Jocelyn. Just be home by dinnertime. Do you need me to pick you up later?"

Of course, she says, like we do this all the time. Like Dad wouldn't flip if he even found out I had a friend.

Do I? Have a friend? Kong's hold was tightening.

Kat breezed into the room with a bowl of chips in one hand, and a plate of cookies in the other. There was a small stack of plastic cups lying alongside the cookies and a 2-liter of diet cola dangling from between two fingers. I gave her the *are you nuts?* look she deserved.

"I could have helped, if I'd known you were provisioning yourself for the winter."

Kat laughed. "The others should be here pretty soon."

"I beg your pardon?"

"Matt's dropping Maddy, Elizabeth, and Heather off, but they had to go do something else first, I don't know. I think Heather has a thing for Matt maybe, but I'm not sure. Do you drink diet?"

"Whatever. I thought we were going to talk about your problem with Marco."

"Yeah, we are."

"Because, I still don't think you understand how serious this is. He knows what you can do."

"I know, Joss. I was there too."

"He's *blackmailing* you!"

"Again, thanks for the recap. Marco is *attempting* to blackmail me."

I dropped my face into my hands. "And I'm *attempting* to clue you in on how bad that is. I told you not to get on his bad side, that you didn't want him to notice you. But you just—"

"I know, I know, you told me so. Noted. Now, moving on, here's the thing about Marco: he's a bully." She dropped the statement with the finality of imparting some great piece of wisdom.

"Duh."

"And the thing with bullies is that they're really cowards. All talk, no action. I mean, what's he ever really *done?* Nothing. Classic bully behavior is to rely on the fact that people feel threatened and capitulate before they ever have to bring about any actual consequences."

Classic bully behavior? Capitulate? I felt like I had just walked into a Psych 101 lecture hall. Then I remembered my dad saying, when they had first moved to Fairview, that Kat's father was the new psych prof at the college. *Lord, save us.*

"Plus, he's just a stupid thug, Joss. We can't let ourselves be afraid of an idiot like that. All we have to do is show him, and everybody else, that he's not all that, he's not so tough, then it's going to be impossible for him to push us or anybody else around any more."

While she was spewing this insanity, I heard the doorbell, voices, footsteps on the stairs, and then the Three Musketeers burst through the door in a fit of giggles that stopped when they saw me. Maybe I have that effect on people. But they were friendly enough and said *hi* to me before they hit Kat's snacky buffet and started making themselves comfortable. I wondered whose seat I was occupying.

"We all hate that chair," Heather said suddenly. When I looked over at her she was taking a long drink of soda.

"I'm surprised Kat got anyone to sit in it. I hope you don't fall on your head."

I looked at Maddy, but it didn't seem like she was making fun of me, exactly. Still, I just wanted to get out of there. It had been over ten years since I'd hung out at a friend's house with other girls my age. I was pretty sure the rules were different now, and I didn't know them. Plus, there's no way to hide in a group of five, especially when you're the novelty.

"So…when is this big party supposed to take place?" Maddy asked..

"Friday night," Kat said. "Boy/girl, obviously."

"I beg your pardon?" It seemed like I was saying that a lot. "Party?"

"For my birthday," Kat said. "It's tomorrow, really, but the party's this weekend."

"Um…oh."

"I can't believe you waited this long to start planning it," Maddy said.

"Nah, my mom's already totally on that. She likes to do parties. All I have to do is invite people. And really, it's Fairview, so not like anyone's got big plans for the weekend. No big."

"True enough. Ok, so who's on the guest list?"

And then they commenced to pretty much list every single person in our class from Angela Mason, cheerleading goddess, down to Rob Grayson, computer geek. I think they even would have invited me, whether I'd been in on this planning session or not. And that begged the question, what *was* I doing there?

"You're coming, right, Joss?" Heather asked.

"I, um…have to ask my Dad…"

"Ask your mom; she likes me," Kat grinned.

I had to smile and roll my eyes at her.

"And of course we'll be asking Dylan, just for you."

I choked on my soda and Heather jumped up to pound me on the back. "Damn, Kat. I hope you plan to be more subtle in the rest of your matchmaking scheme. Give the girl some warning."

"Matchmaking??" I croaked.

"No. Inviting both of you to my party is as far as I'm going with it—"

"Yet!" Maddy coughed into her glove.

"—sort of."

"What does 'sort of' mean?" The edge of hysteria in my voice was so not cool.

"The way I see it," Kat said, "the biggest impediment to your future happiness with Dylan—"

"What makes you think I want future happiness with Dylan??"

"That would be my eyes, dear. Now, as I was saying, your problem, as I see it, is Marco. Marco's pissed off at you for rejecting him, and Dylan can't make his move because Marco's standing between you. The big bully. We get rid of Marco, problem solved. Do you see what I'm saying?"

She was giving me that meaningful look again, and yeah, sort of. But where was she getting all this? How did she know what happened between Marco and me? What made her think that Dylan wanted to make any move? Or that I wanted him to?

Then I pulled my head out of my butt and realized that she was making that up. Kat needed some way to get her friends involved in her problem with Marco. So she was *using* me to do it! She was just making up this nonsense about Dylan and me out of her own curly little head. It was just a coincidence that, yeah, I actually *had* liked him forever, which she couldn't possibly have guessed. Right?

This was no doubt part of my punishment for the whole thing with Trina that had gotten Kat into her mess in the first place. And I still felt so guilty about it that I was inclined to go along with this—even though she was being an idiot and this party didn't have a prayer of helping her. What was a friend supposed to do, beat some sense into her, or support the bad plan? I'd have to go with choice B, for the time being, anyway.

"So, what can we do to put Marco in his place so he stops bothering our friend Joss?"

* * *

Dylan

"I thought you said we were going to do this in the morning. With Rob."

"We will. We'll do it again with Rob, at least once, maybe more before we do the job. I'm just..." Marco rolled his neck and shoulders as we wandered up the chip and soda aisle, "antsy. To get going on this thing. Didn't want to wait for the weekend, and I can't cut anymore school right now."

I grunted. I really didn't want to be here at all. But at least right now, during the after-work/pre-dinner shopping rush, the store was busy and no one noticed two guys wandering around and not picking anything up.

"What's with you lately? You're jumpy, you're pissed off half the time, and you're way too into this *job* that we shouldn't even be thinking about. It's way too complicated and not worth it. It's stupid."

"Hey, I'll decide what's worth it and what's not, all right? You just do what I tell you."

"Since fucking when?" I snarled in a low voice. I was pissed, but not enough not to care about attracting attention. Still, a few women glanced our way and moved off down the aisle.

"Since fucking always. I've always looked out for you. And if I wanted to listen to a lot of nagging, I'd be out with some bitch who would make it worth my while later on."

We had reached the back of the store. "Hold on," I said, and took a few steps over to a stack-out of soda cases. I waited for the last customer to leave the section, pulled a folded piece of paper from my pocket, and "accidentally" dropped it. I bent over behind the soda to pick it up, and when I straightened up I was invisible.

Hopefully no one but Marco had seen me disappear, and we had reasoned in the past that as long as nothing major happened, there was no reason for anyone to be looking at what cameras might have picked up. *Nothing major.* I couldn't figure out why Marco wanted to start that now. For beer? What the hell?

"I've always looked out for you." It was true. And, more and more, I felt like I was paying for that. As kids, it had seemed like we were always equals, two boys who didn't have much good going on at home, running wild, causing trouble and trying not to get caught. Then, when we were nine, Marco did something for me that maybe sparked the change, for both of us. My mom's piece of crap boyfriend had seemed all-powerful to me when he was knocking me around, trying to beat the Talent out of me. When your best friend takes something like that on for you, yeah, it shifts the balance. Makes you grateful. Anything you say, bud. Anything for a friend, right? I guess when a kid takes on something like that, and comes out the winner…I guess that changes him too. That's when Marco really started to believe that the rules just didn't apply to him.

I stood next to him and moved us toward the *Employees Only* door at the back of the store. Standing behind me, no one could see him. He wasn't as tall as I am, and even though he kind of had a wrestler's build, as long as he stood sideways, he was covered. Unlike Rob who was going to have to crouch down somehow—if I didn't get us out of this.

The door swung open, a guy came out wheeling a pallet of cardboard boxes, and Marco and I leapt through the door before it swung shut again. If there had been someone in there, Marco would have to think fast, but I think he liked the possibility of getting to lie when there was no chance of getting into any real trouble.

I grabbed him by the shoulder and walked us over behind a row of pallets stacked high with boxes so I could phase back. As soon as I felt the shift I turned on him.

"That's bullshit—you've always looked out for me. We always looked out for each other. But right now, you're only out for yourself. If this was just gonna be a few cases of beer, we'd get it from Casey's, and then we'd go down to the river and drink it. Old man Casey loses a few cases of beer he wouldn't sell us, but it's not going to ruin him or anything, and it's nothing to the amount of crap his own employees steal from him. No big deal. But you're talking about a truck, disabling security, all this crap. It's not shoplifting anymore, it's honest to God robbery."

"I know."

"Then why are we doing this?"

"Because we can."

I looked into his face, into that meanness in his eyes that had been growing steadily, and let myself process that. Really think about what it meant. It wasn't going to stop here. It was just going to keep getting worse. And so was Marco. He just kept getting meaner, and less like someone I wanted to be around.

That was it. The decision was made. I couldn't stand by him anymore. My gratitude and my patience were all used up.

Friendship over.

"I'm not doing this."

He smiled at me. Actually smiled. "Oh, yes you are."

"No, I'm not. I'm—"

"You're going to do this for me, and anything else I tell you to—"

"Or what? You'll tell my secret? Turn me in?"

"Maybe. Eventually. But before that, I'll tell Joss's."

That got my attention. At first, I didn't even know what he was talking about, and it was just the threat itself. Then I thought about Joss and secrets, and I remembered. How was I always underestimating what he was capable of?

"The fuck you will!"

"She already freaks out if you try to talk to her—or even look at her funny. Imagine what it's going to do to her when everyone knows her dad's batshit crazy. That they had to put him *away* for it." He chuckled. "Then *everyone's* gonna be looking at her funny. Which is just what the freaky bitch deserves."

"Look, you can't do that, ok? That's too fucked up—even for you." It wasn't just about Joss, either. What if this got out and damaged her dad's reputation? What would that do to their business? They didn't have anything else. And while I didn't agree that Joss "freaks out" when people look at her, it was true that she didn't want anyone to notice her. I kinda thought she could handle it, if it came down to it, but then, I just didn't want her to have to.

"It's really not. So here's the deal: you and I go on like this conversation never happened. You do what I tell you to do until this thing is done, and quit giving me shit about it. And I'll keep my mouth shut about your girlfriend's crazy dad. Deal?"

I didn't answer him. He knew the answer.

"Now get me out of here. I've got stuff to do."

CHAPTER 8

Joss

Tuesday was family dinner night. Dad closed the store around six, and we were usually eating by seven. Part of what Jilly used to like about it was that it meant she could stay up a little later on Tuesdays. Now that it was all old hat, she had been campaigning that family dinner night become family pizza night. Yeah, good luck with that.

"Jill, stop playing with those peas and eat them or no TV tonight," Dad said. Wouldn't be family dinner night if he didn't, I guess.

Whining followed.

"I had a visit from Pete Connolly today," Dad announced, out of nowhere. This explained his slightly elevated level of agitation. In a family where everyone is on hyper-alert for things to go horribly wrong, subtleties are often easy to spot. Mr. Connolly was one of Dad's cop buddies—or one of the cops who frequented the shop, whom Dad kissed up to, but secretly loathed as part of the "police state this country has become," or whatever. So what we were about to hear was going to be cop-shop gossip. Dad never was one for idle gossip, so this was probably going to suck. "He's pissed off because he went out on a call last night where a cop was injured, and they've put out a gag order on everyone, and are keeping it out of the media."

"What happened?" Mom asked.

"Dumbass kid blew it. Phil Meeks. You know him, Joss?"

"He's in a few of my classes, average grades, hangs out with some other trailer park kids, mostly."

"Not for long. Dumbass kid. Lives with his mother and her boyfriend—I got the impression it wasn't the first time Connolly had been there. Anyway, this time they get there, the boyfriend was belligerent, big surprise, arguing with them, lying, and the woman yanks one of those moving water picture things off the wall—pretty hefty— and cracks the boyfriend in the side of the head with it. Right in front of the cops, so now they've got to take her in for assault. She resists, they're trying to restrain her, and then all hell breaks loose.

"Seems the kid, Phil, had been watching all of this go down. They knew he was there, but he's not a big kid, not threatening at all, and he was staying well out of their way. Next thing you know, Connolly says it was like a science fiction movie. Streaks of red light, things bursting into flame…They all got the hell out of there and the damn thing burned to the ground."

"I read about a mobile home fire in the paper today," Mom said. "The article didn't give much detail, but it said the place was a total loss, no one was hurt, and the cause of the fire was 'under investigation'."

"According to Connolly, one of the cops got hit in the arm, burned through his clothes and down into his skin. He's in the hospital, but no one's allowed to talk about it. No doubt because they have to wait and see what the Feds want to do about the kid. Connolly's pissed that they didn't even take him into custody, but how're they going to hold a kid with laser vision? They're not equipped."

Laser vision? Phil?

Mom shook her head. "So they just left him running loose?"

Dad and I both glared at her.

"Now, don't you two look at me like that. Clearly, this boy is dangerous." There's no point in arguing with any of Mom's statements marked 'clearly'. "Do they know where

Phil is now? How long does Mr. Connolly think it will be before the agents arrive?"

"This is what's really pissing him off. He was told that no one would be here until this weekend, and the cops are supposed to 'just keep an eye on the kid' until then. He's staying with a friend's family in the park right now, and we'll see what happens when and if his mother gets released. I think they may try to hold her without bail just to ensure he stays local."

Mom shook her head.

"Goes without saying, Joss, that I want you to stay in this weekend," Dad said.

I was about to roll my eyes at him, like *duh, where would I go on the weekend?* Then I remembered Kat's party. Well, if he told me I couldn't go, I guess I wouldn't be too upset about it.

"Um, Dad, and I say this totally hearing what you're saying, but my—that is…there's this party Friday night that—"

"A party?! Joan, did you know anything about this?" Dad's color was up. I was wishing I'd just told Kat they said no without even asking. And at the same time, it was suddenly becoming really important to me that they say yes. And what was that all about?

"No, honey, I didn't. Joss, tell us about this party. Whose party is it?"

"Um, well, it's not a big deal, I mean—"

"Jilly-bug, go watch TV," Dad said.

Jill looked down at the peas on her plate and back at us. Then she took off.

My mom gave me her *I asked you a question* look.

"Kat Dawson's birthday party. She…I only started talking to her because I was struggling in Chem, and I know that being below average attracts attention, so I asked her some questions. And I guess she felt like that was

75

grounds for inviting me to her party. I mean, it's not a big deal at all. She's inviting pretty much everyone, from what I heard, and it seems like everyone's going. Not that that means I have to go, unless it would be weird if I didn't." I shut my mouth. It wasn't like me to babble, even at home. Dad was looking stern but otherwise unreadable. Mom was looking at me like we were sharing a secret.

"Well, Gene, she does have a point. A girl can stand out by being a loner as much as by being popular."

"You know why we discourage her about getting too friendly at that school."

"I know, darling. And Joss knows too. I think she's done wonderfully well at following your guidance so far. If she wants to go to this party, or if she just wants to not have to explain why she didn't go, I think we should trust her. How do you feel about that, Jocelyn?"

Sometimes I wonder if my mom had some kind of shrink training in the past, or if it was just being exposed to so many around my dad when I was little.

"I, um, think it could be ok. I mean, I'm old enough where it would be kind of weird for me to try to explain that I wasn't allowed to go to a birthday party. Other kids do that stuff all the time. But it's not that I want to, it's— like mom said—it's hard to explain why if I don't go. I mean, if I say I just don't want to, then that's a dig on Kat, and I don't want her—or her friends—getting mad at me, because that just gets them talking about you, you know? Plus, there's going to be so many other kids there, it will be just like at school: easy for me to blend into the background."

"Gene, I think Joss has clearly shown that she's trustworthy enough to go to this party."

Clearly.

* * *

Joss

"It's too bad you couldn't stay for dinner last night."

I glanced around to see if anyone was taking notice of the fact that Kat was pulling me along the hall with her. Of course they weren't. Kids get really wrapped up in their own stuff so that even someone like me hanging around someone like Kat doesn't penetrate. Which was good.

"It was family dinner night."

"Oh yeah? That's cute. So after you left, we worked out our whole plan to get Marco, the dick."

"About that...Kat, it's just not a good idea."

"You haven't even heard the plan yet."

"I don't need to. Your logic is completely flawed. I mean, I guess if Marco were a textbook bully, like you said, then maybe. But he's not how you said, and there's no way he's going to back down because of whatever public humiliation you guys come up with. If anything, it's only going to make him mad, and you're just going to make things worse."

"I'm telling you, this is a solid plan, Joss. You've got to stop worrying."

Yeah, right. We stopped at Kat's locker and I let my head bang against the wall as she spun her combination.

"So, here's what we came up with. It turns out—"

"No," I interrupted, firmly. "I don't want any part of this—not even being in on it."

"Really? You don't even want to *know*? 'Cause it's kinda juicy gossip."

"No. Really."

Kat shrugged as she pulled out her backpack. "Suit yourself. And so ungrateful," she said airily, smiling, "since it's really all for you."

That again. "Yeah, about that..."

"What the hell is this?"

For a second I thought she was talking to me. Like the fact that I might actually say something about how she'd used me, and twisted the truth into a pretzel to get her friends in on her game, was somehow shocking to her. But she was spilling the contents of a manila envelope into her hand.

On the top of the stack was a type-written letter, business style, and the addressee was *National Institutes for Ability Control* followed by the address of NIAC's main office in DC. I got as far as *To Whom It May Concern* before Kat shifted the letter to the bottom of the pile. Under that was a picture of Krista. Not a portrait, a candid shot where she wasn't looking at the camera. As I looked closer, it seemed blurry and like she wasn't aware of being photographed.

Then I saw it.

"Jesus."

"What?" Kat asked.

I just put my finger on the part of the picture where Krista's arm, extended toward a glass on the table near her, was just a little too long and too thin in the lower half. Just a little. It was obvious she was reaching for the glass, and yet as I looked more carefully at the picture, it also wasn't obvious because she wasn't leaning in that direction at all. It was just that slightly too-long arm extended toward the glass.

"Am I seeing what I think I'm seeing?"

"What's next?" I snapped.

The next photo showed Krista standing in front of a closet, reaching for something up high. Her body seemed longer and thinner than it should have been, the elements of the room strangely short and chunky by comparison. Out of proportion to what my brain wanted to see.

Kat started leafing through the stack. There were only a few, more of the same kinds of moments. Moments when Krista assumed no one was looking.

"Do you think these were…manipulated?"

I thought about what a good athlete Krista was, and how much easier it must be to get to that tennis ball on time if you could get your racket just a little closer while your body caught up. I thought about how it must help in the last moments of a sprint if you could make your legs just a little bit longer.

Jesus. Out loud I said, "No, I don't. Kat, you have *got* to pay him off."

Kat flipped back to the letter and we scanned through it. An anonymous citizen, claiming to do his part and obey the law, blah blah. Part of me was seething with rage over the letter, the law, Krista's carelessness—But I shoved it down because that didn't do any good, and I had plenty of pure freak-out to keep my brain occupied anyway.

"No way. See, this is exactly what I'm saying. Look how cowardly this is. Pictures through a window, anonymous letter. What if he's done this before, Joss? If I give in to him, he's just going to keep doing it again and again, and who knows how many people will get hurt. I *have* to stand up to him. I just have to."

"But—" Phil Meeks was walking down the hall, on his way out of the building, no doubt. I had this wild urge to grab him and shake him until he agreed to get out of town. But I was rooted to the spot. My association with Kat, which seemed by turns both voluntary and involuntary, was risky enough—too risky since she was bent on being an idiot. I just couldn't risk more than one clueless blockhead at a time. When I'd seen him in Math, I couldn't believe he was still around. Didn't he think what he did would get him reported? Didn't he think they were coming for him? Why didn't he just tie a bow around his neck while he waited?

I half expected NIAC agents—possibly in riot gear or something—to come storming in after him at any moment.

"Hey." I just about jumped out of my skin as someone banged into the lockers behind me. I whirled around and looked up to find Dylan towering over me. I automatically took a step back, bumping into Kat. It was like dancing in a crowded club. I assume. She covered for me by shutting her locker and, you know, talking.

"Hey, Dylan. Fancy meeting you here."

"Um, yeah… your note said: Come by my locker after school—gotta ask you something."

What the hell, they're passing notes? Damn, voice in my head needs to cool it.

"Well, who knew if you actually would?"

"Kat, does anyone ever tell you 'no'?"

No.

"Actually no," she grinned, tossing curls like there was no tomorrow. "So I'll just tell you: you're coming to my party Friday night. My house. Seven o'clock. And tell your…*posse* or whatever."

"All of them?"

"Yeah," she said in the tone of *Duh.* "*Everyone's* coming."

"Yeah, all right. Thanks."

"Oh, hang on, I made maps." She started dialing her combo again.

"So, 'everyone' mean you're going too, Joss?"

But I hadn't remembered how to talk yet.

"Of course she is," Kat covered, rummaging. I had this strange feeling of Kat-love sweep over me just then.

"Do you…need a ride?"

"I, um…I'm actually going home with Kat after school on Friday. To help her set up and stuff." Kat elbowed me in the kidney and I had to not yelp. *She'd best not be laughing.*

"Oh, well, cool. I guess I'll see you there then."

My heart was pounding away this whole time. The conversation we'd had in the store was longer, more personal even, kinda. But this was the second time Dylan had talked to me in the same *month*. And yeah, he was just killing time while Kat looked for her maps—as if Kat didn't know exactly where they were. I felt a lot of my Kat-love evaporate.

"Sure."

Kat finally found her flyers and handed one to Dylan. They bantered a little more, and I was stuck standing between them like an idiot, saying nothing, studying the creases in the sleeves of Dylan's leather jacket. He finally said bye, so I had to look up and say bye, and he was smiling at us, which must have been for Kat, and I almost stuttered over my whole syllable. Man, I was in a bad way and needed to stuff this stupid crush thing before I made a total ass out of myself.

He turned and walked down the hall, which I was really busy watching until Kat shoved me so hard from behind that I stumbled forward.

"You big dork!"

"What?"

"My mom will be taking *us* to the store for last minute snacks and whatever when she picks *us* up on Friday."

"Okay."

"I can't believe you did that. He was totally going to take you to the party!"

"He asked if I needed a ride. That is *so* not the same thing."

"Yes. It is."

"No, it's not. Dylan likes my dad's store. And he's probably been in there enough Friday nights—like every other guy in this town with nothing better to do—to know that it's usually both my parents in the store on Fridays."

"That scenario seems to have him paying a lot of attention to how your family works…"

Yeah, maybe so. "Then he was being nice. Which is because he's a nice guy, not because he's being nice to me in particular."

"Sure…I'll bet he's going around making carpool arrangements for the whole class."

"Oh shut up."

"It's too bad he's got such lousy taste in friends though."

Yeah. Really

CHAPTER 9

Dylan

The whole thing with Joss and Kat was weird. In a good way, though. I'd been in school with Joss since kindergarten and while I don't really remember back that far, I don't ever remember her being buddy-buddy with anyone. I never really thought anything bad about her for being a loner. It's a valid lifestyle choice, I guess. But it was cool to see Kat kind of—I don't know—taking her under her wing or whatever.

If she started talking to Kat, maybe she'd start talking to me sometime.

Hey, it could happen.

If I thought I was thinking about her a lot before, man, since Marco and his damn threats at the store, Joss was pretty much all I was thinking about. I thought maybe she kind of liked me too. Especially talking to her and Kat about the party. Joss is quiet, but usually when she has to talk to people, she's pretty direct, looks them in the eye, says what she has to say, and walks away. Not rude, just— that's how she is. But just now she seemed kind of shy. Yeah, she didn't take me up on my lame offer to take her to the party, but I hadn't really expected her to.

Maybe it was kind of stupid of me to be wandering around thinking about whether or not Joss was interested in me, or to be having all kinds of fantasies about how she would react when she somehow found out about my pact with Marco, and what I had been willing to do to protect her. This big *my hero* moment was building up in my head. Not like that's why I was doing it. I just felt this need to look out for her, whether she ever knew it or not. But if she

83

ever found out and felt the need to throw herself at me, I figured I'd catch her.

But yeah, kind of dumb to be thinking about stuff like that when I was on my way to Crime Practice. I had gotten in way over my head, and I had to find some way to get out of this dumbass plan of Marco's without giving him a reason to ruin Joss, and without landing my ass in jail or State School.

Down along the river, there are a number of abandoned old buildings. Crumbling brick, some with whole walls missing, a lot of them completely obscured from view by trees and stuff, and some could only be reached on foot. There was some reason for it, something to do with the changing economy, the railroad, I don't know, but it had left all these early 1900s factories—whatever they'd been—still standing, forgotten, along the river.

One of these was our hangout, even though it was across town from school and a hike to get there. I'd missed my chance to get a ride with Eric, so I was stuck walking. Like I said, it should have been strategizing time, but…

When I walked in, Jeff was smoking and kicking a wall that still had some plaster, watching it crumble. Eric was reading a car magazine, and it looked like Rob was doing his homework.

"Hey, guys. Where's Marco?"

"Detention," Jeff answered, looking at his watch. "Shouldn't be much longer, though."

"You guys hear about Kat's party?" *Way to prioritize.* And once I got that topic started, it went along on its own for a few minutes, while Marco's arrival got closer. Finally I just broke in with, "What do you guys think about this plan?"

"I think Eric ought to pick me up first instead of you," Jeff said.

"Not that," *you moron.* "The beer thing."

I had everyone's attention, though only Rob was openly showing it. They all knew I was against this, and Rob would be smart enough to really want me to get us out of it. If I could just convince Eric and Jeff to back out, Marco would have to recruit them all over again. Maybe that would be too much effort for beer.

"What about it?" Eric asked, flipping a page.

"Doesn't it seem kind of…complicated to you? I mean, why are we doing this? The whole thing with Rob and me sneaking around cameras and disabling alarm systems—it's total overkill. What if we miss something? Something that gets us all caught? What if we end up in jail over this—or worse?"

"Hey, you freaks worry about going to State School. Not me! Just plain ol' Jeff here. Sucks to be you."

"Shut the hell up," Eric drawled, pitching a piece of crumbled brick that intentionally missed Jeff's head and bounced off the wall.

"But you're fine with a criminal record," I said.

"We're still minors."

"Oh, great attitude. Come on guys, if this is just about beer, it's just not worth it."

"You're right, Dylan." It happened really fast. I had seen the warning look flash across Rob's face before he ducked his head, but I processed it about the same time I heard Marco's voice and felt his hand clamp, kind of painfully, on my shoulder. "It's not worth it, *just for beer.* It's good that you're here, looking out for the team's interests. And your concern has showed me that it's time to let you all in on the rest of the plan."

He shook me by the shoulder before he walked away, and I was trying to find my balance in every sense as he strode into the room and climbed up to his usual perch on the deep, concrete sill of a glassless window.

"You got me. I lied. I'm not *really* after beer, although I'm sure we'll still lift a few cases. But there's not much difference between the plan I laid out for you the other day and what I've been working on. When Dylan and I were in the store yesterday, I got the information I needed to figure out the rest of it."

"Spit it out already," Eric drawled, bored. "What are you after?"

"The bank vault."

I leaned back against the wall, letting it hold me up. All I could think was *Felony*. I glanced at Rob who looked like he might vomit.

Jeff made a show of dropping his cigarette and stomping it out, the action looking a lot like a toddler stamping his foot. "Why didn't I know about this?" Figures Jeff's main problem with the plan would be that Marco didn't let him in on it before everyone else.

Marco ignored him and looked to Eric, whose face was unreadable. Eric just said, "Go on."

"The plan is pretty much the same, as far as Rob and Dylan getting in and staying hidden until after closing. They take care of the alarms and the cameras. All of them. After Dylan and I finished up yesterday, I waited behind and chatted up one of the bank chicks. I got all the information we need about the bank procedures, security, and how the lock on the vault works. Rob, you shouldn't have any trouble with it."

Rob opened his mouth to say something but choked on it.

"You're basing a fucking bank robbery on information you got flirting with a grocery store bank teller? Are you out of your fucking mind??" I never knew plain stupidity could piss me off that much.

"No. This is the plan, Dylan," he said calmly and like he was talking to a moron, which I was starting to realize he actually was. "It's my plan, and you're all in it with me. I don't want to hear any more complaining or second-guessing. You're the one who's putting us all at risk by trying to divide us, undermine everyone's confidence. This is going to be fucking great for all of us—as long as nobody fucks it up. And if they do, it's because you're worrying them like a fucking grandmother. So cut it out. You and I just talked about this *yesterday*, and *yesterday* you were on board. Do you remember that?"

I gritted my teeth, knowing his emphasis on "yesterday" referred to his threats against Joss.

"Yes."

"And…has anything changed since yesterday?"

"No."

"Then you're still with us. Come on. I want to hear you say it."

"Yeah. I'm in." Rob was looking at me like I was a total traitor.

"Good, then before we start working with you and Rob, let's go over the details I got from *Mon-i-ca*."

But I couldn't really pay attention. Rob would. He'd remember it all. He was too scared not to, and I was too busy thinking about what an idiot I was.

If I'd realized—no, that's not even right. If I'd accepted what was right in front of my face for the last few years, if I'd just parted ways with Marco when he started acting like a total ass…I had been in total denial, thinking that he'd get over it and go back to being my cool friend I used to have fun with. I kept thinking I had to cut him some slack because his mom was gone and it was just him and his dad, and his dad wasn't so great and whatever. And that if I just stood by him and kept being his friend, he'd snap out of it. How do you snap out of being an asshole? I had been making excuses for him—for years! And that's why I was in over my head right now.

Yeah, some hero I was, waiting around while Marco droned on with details, so I could practice for my new career as a felon. And the thing was, it never crossed my mind to walk away, knowing that Joss would be hurt. Because that was my fault too. I never should have forgotten what Marco knew about her dad, and I never should have let him know that I was interested in her. The thing with her dad—that was probably why she tried so hard not to let anyone notice her. And after all those years of her walking on eggshells, I decide I just *have* to start talking to her, and manage to shove her right in front of the wolf.

All I could do now was stand up and stay between them.

CHAPTER 10

Joss

I figured Kat's party to be at about two-third's swing. This was a completely arbitrary judgment as this was my first party since I was five. I was going by the fact that everyone seemed to be there, music was pumping out of the speakers out on the deck, people were talking in small groups, and it was mostly girls inside, in the family room, pretending they weren't watching most of the guys, who were outside, on the deck that opened off of it.

Then Marco came in with his crew and headed for the buffet of snacks Kat and I had spent the afternoon working on. Kat and I had been standing at the table for a bit, while Kat displayed some rabid perfectionist tendencies I wasn't aware she had. But of course I should have guessed. After she and her friends had strong-armed me into a mini-makeover and ridiculous clothes, she had kept me in her hip-pocket so far this evening, making sure I didn't revert to form, she said. She was fussing over neatly folded napkins that were obviously destined to go unused when Heather nudged her and inclined her head toward the door. The girls immediately went on alert, and so did I. They turned as one, preparing to strike, while I casually began to back away from them, heading for the corner I'd been longing for.

As if my heart weren't pounding hard enough, from the people, the noise, from knowing something was about to happen, Dylan's glance caught mine, and he smiled at me. I tried not to glance down at myself, at the scoop-neck top they'd made me wear that hugged me all over, and the sparkly little pendant that said *hey, we got some cleavage*

89

over here! Most people probably wouldn't consider it low cut at all, but this was probably the most clavicle I had ever displayed. I crossed my arms over my chest, realized that probably made the cleavage thing worse, uncrossed them, and shifted uncomfortably in Kat's girl-shoes.

"Marco," Kat said, grabbing a cup of soda from the table behind her. "I'm really glad you could come to my party."

He looked suspicious as she exchanged his empty cup for the full one. This was further proof, in my opinion, that Marco wasn't as stupid as Kat thought he was. *"Know your enemy."* My dad's words went through my head. I had tried one last time to talk Kat out of whatever it was they had planned, but she wasn't hearing it. She was convinced that a Psych 101 textbook put everyone into their neat little boxes. But how could it? I wondered what Psych 101 had to say about minds that could cause temporary blindness, move objects, start fires.

"Well thanks. That's really nice of you. Although I hope you're not thinking that this changes anything between us. If you know what I'm saying."

"What are you guys talking about?" Jeff asked.

"About how Kat wants me, but I told her it wouldn't work between us. Isn't that right, Kat?"

"You're hilarious." To give her credit, Kat seemed perfectly comfortable sparring with Marco, even though more of the other kids were sensing something was going on that was worth paying attention to. "I think you and I got off on the wrong foot. I mean, there's so much we don't know about each other. Like, for example, I didn't know that it's just you and your dad at home."

All conversation stopped. Outside, the music was as loud as ever, but all eyes were on the two groups facing off in Kat's family room. Kat, Maddy, Heather, and Elizabeth vs. Marco, Dylan, Jeff, and Eric.

"So? What of it?"

"I'm just saying that I didn't know it. I'm sure it's been hard on you."

"So, what's this? You're going to pretend to feel all sorry for me because my mom ran off and we don't know where she is? Don't bother. We don't care."

"Ran off? You mean 'was taken away,' right? 'Cause your mom's at Hellermann's, right?"

"Shut up, Kat," Jeff snapped. "You don't know what you're talking about. His mom's no mental—"

Marco jabbed Jeff in the ribs. "Who told you that?"

I fell back against the wall, so grateful that I wasn't a part of this, and that no one was paying attention to me right now. And at the same time, I felt guilty because I could have been in the loop. Maybe I could have stopped this. Because this was wrong. Even to Marco, it was just wrong. My dad had spent time at the R.K. Hellermann Center for Mental Health. I wasn't ashamed of it, but…damn.

"After our…conversation the other day, I just wanted to find out as much about you as I could. So I did."

"Who. Told you that. About my mother?"

Dylan stepped up, "I don't know what's going on between the two of you, but making stuff up like this? It's messed up, Kat."

When you spend your time watching life, you read a lot of people, and here's what I was pretty sure about: what Kat just said was true, it was news to Jeff and Eric, and Dylan was pissed off.

"But I'm not making it up, am I, Marco?"

"Kat," Dylan's voice was more forceful this time. "You need to back off. This isn't you."

"No, hey, it's fine." Marco stepped forward. I think Kat wanted to step back, but didn't. "I mean, what does it really matter what people think? So either my mom's a dead-beat ho or she's a freakin' lunatic. What's the difference, right?"

Kat shrugged. "I guess the difference is something like: are you so obnoxious that you made your mom run away, or did you drive her insane?"

Dylan clapped a hand on Marco's shoulder. "Come on, man, let's go."

"Oh no, we're not leaving. Not when Kat and I are really getting to know each other."

* * *

Joss

"Are you okay?"

I glanced up at Dylan and then immediately found a focus point on his shoulder. It was lame that I could never seem to look this boy in the eye. Kat's mom had called her, which was nice for her, since it gave her an excuse to quit while she was sort of ahead. She'd breezed out of the room, her entourage in her wake. Dylan had led Marco outside for some air, and the rest of his crew had followed. I was surprised that I hadn't seen him come back. I was way too much in my head.

"Shouldn't you be asking your friend that question?"

"I am," he replied, completely throwing me. After he let that sink in for a beat, he kept going. "If you mean Marco, he's Marco. He's either ok or he's not, and he's not going to talk about it here, if anywhere."

I nodded.

"So I was thinking that maybe…I mean, I noticed that you looked…"

"What?" Between the guilt and the shoes I was damned uncomfortable and it came out defensive.

"Upset, I guess."

Why are you noticing how I look, or anything about me? You are seriously toying with the Laws of the Universe, you know that, right?

"Yeah, well, it was an upsetting scene. And one I didn't know anything about," I added quickly.

"I'm sure you didn't."

Maybe that's part of what I liked about Dylan, beyond the shoulders and the blue eyes. He was always trying to smooth things over, make people feel better, and he usually seemed sincere about it.

Still, I found myself babbling, "I mean it. I mean, I knew there was some bad blood or whatever between Marco and Kat, and I knew she had some kind of plan to get back at him, but I swear, I did not know what it—"

"Joss," he reached out and touched my shoulder. I jumped—I couldn't help it—and he dropped his hand quickly. "I know you didn't know. You wouldn't be a part of something like that. It's not your style."

I almost said something biting, like "How would you know?" Something to push him back because I was feeling very literally cornered. But I didn't. Instead I went with, "I didn't think it was hers either. Now I don't know what to think."

"I didn't realize there was anything going on between the two of them, and I'm not pretending to know what's going on. But I can say that Marco's not an easy person to get along with, especially lately. Sometimes he…makes people do things. Things they know are wrong, things they never would have believed they'd do."

"What are you talking about?"

I looked up again and he wasn't really focused on me at all, but my question brought his eyes back to mine.

"Nothing really." He smiled, but I wasn't thrown by it this time.

"I thought Marco was your friend."

"A lot of people think that. I did too. Never mind," he said, shrugging it off and turning to go, "I was just—"

I grabbed his sleeve, and we both froze, looking at my hand. For a minute I thought that maybe he understood how crazy it was. I didn't touch people. I *encouraged* people to leave me alone. And I still wasn't letting him go.

There was a whole jumble of things going on in my head. I was kind of feeling this growing like for him—as a person and not just a pair of shoulders—the longer we talked. I was actually feeling concerned about him, and even though I usually hated the feeling, I wanted to know more about Dylan. And about this problem he was hinting at between him and Marco. If he was. The pink frilly haze of *omg, he's really talking to me* was hard to think through.

He sighed. "It's no big deal. He's just…not who he used to be, and I've been noticing it a lot more lately." He paused, and the self-deprecating half smile he gave me made my heart trip. "He's been giving you a hard time for the last few years, Joss. This is the part where you call me an ass because I'm just now figuring this out."

"Sometimes it's easy to ignore things you don't want to deal with. Even if they're right in front of you."

"Is it?" He had turned back to face me, and suddenly his question seemed really personal. My pulse was pounding harder than the music, and you'd think some of that blood would be going to my racing, light-headed brain, but it must have been all in my red face instead. I was definitely over-analyzing.

A loud, authoritative voice boomed in the room's wide entry. "If Phillip Meeks is here, we need him to identify himself and come forward."

CHAPTER 11

Joss

"Who's asking?" Phil had been standing behind the couch, leaning over Jessica Morgan and looking at a magazine she was holding. He could have dropped to the floor behind the sofa, but instead he actually walked around it and swaggered forward, his hands in his pockets.

I nearly dropped my face into my hands. *The moron! Some people just cannot be helped.* I had to wonder if I was one of them since I found myself moving slowly toward Kat, who had placed herself in the middle of the room, between the adults and Phil. My instinct should have been to back farther into my corner, to stay as unnoticed as possible. But I didn't want to see Kat make the same mistake twice. Worse.

"National Institutes for Ability Control." Both of the men standing with Kat's parents, dressed in loose-fitting black clothes from head to toe, flashed ID cards. "We're authorized to take you in under suspicion that you possess an unreported Ability—"

"Get out of my house. Dad, tell them they're not taking anyone."

"Kathryn…"

"This isn't a matter that concerns you, Miss Dawson. We're just here for the boy."

Kat started a speech about Constitutional rights and such that I didn't even listen to. I did a quick scan as I moved carefully toward the center of the room. The agent who wasn't speaking glanced at me, but I wasn't the only one moving. I could feel Dylan just behind me. Other kids were slipping out through the sliding doors. I saw Jeff and Marco vault over the deck rail and others slipping away into the night. The agents didn't seem to care, as long as they had their quarry in their sights.

We had the two agents standing in the doorway between the family room and formal living area. I saw two others enter the lighted part of the yard, slinking smoothly toward us. The only other exit was the swinging door I had been standing near moments ago, which led to the kitchen. I wondered if agents would be coming through there at any moment. I wondered why I hadn't used it myself.

The other girls were now standing beside Kat. *Great,* I thought, *ready to jump right into her next stupid plan.* As soon as I reached her, I put a restraining hand on her arm. She hardly noticed. Dylan moved silently around to stand in front of me, and I had to lean into Kat a little just to be able to see something besides his shoulder.

"Come on now, son. Let's not make this difficult," the agent said to Phil.

"Difficult how?" Phil asked. "You mean like this?"

His eyes turned bright red, glowed, and then a beam of red light shot up to the ceiling. It popped with a little burst of flame and rained plaster down on the agents. Everyone jumped back, someone screamed, and then the room seemed to freeze.

"That's it. We need everyone on the ground, now!" The agents drew weapons, but they were just Tasers. They'd hurt like hell, incapacitate, but they probably wouldn't kill anyone. I wasn't so sure about Phil. Still, as much of a dumbass as Phil was, he was kindred, a Talent, and these guys were jack-booted thugs. No way I was lying down to make their jobs easier.

While some of the kids, and even Kat's parents, hit the carpet, I was surprised that there were a lot of us still standing. I felt Kat gather herself to do something, and I squeezed her arm.

"Don't even think about it," I hissed in her ear.

The agents were still yelling, at Phil, at everyone, demanding compliance.

"Someone has to do something!" she hissed back.

And then it happened. So fast. The lead agent took aim at Phil, pulled back on the trigger, and I just reacted, flinging out that invisible line in my mind like a whip, wrapping it around the weapon, yanking hard. What everyone saw was the gun flipping out of his hand and landing on the carpet several feet away. The electrodes meant for Phil pinged harmlessly against the stone fireplace.

Phil was reacting too, though, this time aiming his vision at the agent and hitting him in the shoulder. The man screamed, clamping a hand over the spurt of flame from his clothing and dropping to the ground. The other three agents, also unable to hold onto their weapons, rushed toward Phil.

I held onto Kat as she started forward, but saw Matt and Maddy rush in. Maddy threw herself on the back of one of the agents. She pressed her cheek to his, like she was bracing for a struggle, but then slid off when Matt grabbed his arm and stared at him.

When Matt dropped his hand, the agent simply turned and started to leave.

And that's when the dolls started to move.

It started with just one. A little French number in a blue bonnet that only caught my eye because it was on the mantle, right near where Phil was struggling with the two agents. One of them had him in a headlock and had drawn some kind of metallic bag over his head while the other tried to hold him still from the side. I watched, fascinated, as the little figure with the blonde ringlets picked up a decorative plate and swung it at Headlock Guy. Two more plates followed in rapid succession, shards of china flying up when the plates—which weren't flung with too much force—bounced off the agents and struck the fireplace.

But it was enough to freak them out.

They stumbled back from Phil, reaching for the heavy artillery they had worn slung across their backs, and they both aimed at the fireplace.

"Rubber bullets!" Maddy shouted at the room that was erupting into another round of terrified screams, "Get down!"

Part of my mind was trying to process all this, even as I reached out to the table legs with my mind and dumped the contents of the buffet onto the floor. I slid it into position in front of us as a shield, barely missing Dylan who was already tugging me to the floor behind it. I pulled the couch that had been near the back door, only to find there had been kids behind it. They bolted outside, and then Phil hurled himself over the table and Dylan had to pull me out of his path.

I couldn't even appreciate it. I was too busy, my mind throwing out its lines, grabbing furniture and building up our wall, the huge pieces flying toward us and stacking, my mind racing and working so hard that there was nothing else but finding and stacking pieces until a hand clamped onto my shoulder.

"We need a plan, Joss. What do we do next?"

I checked my need to gather the air in front of Matt into a burst that would knock him on his ass and settled for a glare and a hiss: "Get out of my head!" Which I then realized there was no way he could hear over the shouting and gunfire.

"Just listen. Heather says to tell you to figure out how we're going to get out of here. You're the only one who can." I tried to shake him off, opening my mouth to say something, but he must have read my face—I hoped it was

my face he was reading. *"I don't know why she says that, but she just knows things."*

Dylan's arm came around, giving Matt the shove I'd wanted to and making him let go of me. "What the hell, Matt?" he yelled, but I think I was the only one who could hear. Matt just shook his head.

We didn't have time for this. Heather was right, someone needed to figure a way out of here. I had built up our little corral with three walls and the fourth being the kitchen doorway. Years of training from my dad had made thinking to include an escape route automatic, as well the thought of how I'd block it if it were compromised. Now I wondered if anyone was beyond the door, and Heather jumped into my view, shaking her head violently.

No, I thought, *don't go that way?*

She looked exasperated and started climbing over kids to get to me. At the same time, the agents began to body-slam my furniture wall, and I diverted my attention to holding it steady and keeping a wing-back chair from falling on Elizabeth's head. I wanted to call out to her, but she was oblivious, and through the opening she was watching from I could see once-pretty dolls with disheveled clothing and missing limbs tearing at the agents and being shattered by rubber bullets.

"Kitchen's clear! I think!" she yelled right in my ear.

You think?

I scuttled to the door to check, but Dylan grabbed me before I could push it open and looked at me like I was out of my mind. Then he slipped through without another word.

Boys. Idiots.

He came right back and practically dragged me through. I saw Matt darting around touching everyone for a brief moment before they turned and headed for the kitchen too. Because I'm just that paranoid, I waited until a few people were through before I slid the refrigerator in front of the door that led off to the rest of the house. *Nope, can't pin that on me.*

When Eric dragged Kat through the swinging door and everyone was in kitchen, I visualized my wall outside and pulled as much of it in toward the kitchen as I could. It's hard for me to move what I can't see, so most of it I just let fall and it was enough for now.

"But my parents—"

"They don't want your parents," I interrupted Kat. "They're cooperating, and these guys are obviously supposed to use non-lethal force. So don't worry about them, ok? We need to know how to get out of here. What's out that way?"

"But—"

"The garage," Maddy supplied. "There are a few steps down, but it opens right into the two-car garage."

I remembered that now. I'd come in that way twice already. I'd hated the drills my dad had put me through, the prolonged, vigorous use of my ability, or using it under distracting conditions. But it was the only way I was able to do it now while I was trying to hold the doors, figure out our next moves, and trying not to think about all the Talents I was seeing in people I had been going to school with my whole life.

"Of course." I looked at Heather who had known there was no one in the kitchen. Would she know about the garage too? She gave me a thumbs up. What Matt said flitted through my head, that thing about Heather thinking *I* was the one who could figure a way out of this. *That girl is out of her freakin' mind.*

Everyone was watching me or the door. Heather twirled her finger at her head in the universal crazy sign before pointing to herself, smirking at me the whole time.

Bitch was reading my mind!

She mimed an offended expression and the hallway door started to give way. I hadn't been paying enough attention. I panicked, knocked over the fridge, took the range next to it and flipped it on top. I heard someone—Matt, maybe—say, "Holy shit! Who's doing that?" Belatedly, I noticed that it was an electric range, thank God.

Heather already had the door open, and I shouted at everyone to get down into the garage. As soon as their backs were all turned, I started pulling the cabinets from the walls. I went last, Dylan trying to tear my arm from the socket, the invisible strings to my mind pulling them all with me into a stack against the door as I slammed it closed.

Now what? I'll figure out what's next just as soon as I throw up. My head was pounding with the stress and effort as I literally stumbled down the steps.

"Ok, everybody just calm down," I said. "We're doing great. We've got trained government agents out there, and a few Talent kids just showed them their asses." Someone whooped. Dad always said that morale's important. Not everything, not at the expense of reality, but if you don't believe in yourself or your team, you've probably lost already. "Now, it's Phil they're after. We have to get him out of here. I wish I knew how many there are…"

"There are the four agents in the house," Maddy said, "and there were supposed to be two more in the backyard for backup. But they didn't come in at the signal, so they might be incapacitated—"

"What signal?"

"Radio signal." Maddy held up her hand to shut me up. "There are four more agents in two cars, waiting to give chase if—"

"Did someone say 'chase'?" Eric asked, grinning.

"Quit kidding around," Dylan snapped.

101

"Who's kidding? Look at this baby." Eric ran his hand across the top of Kat's dad's Corvette. "I don't care what they're driving, they'll never catch this."

"They're driving Crown Vics," Maddy said.

Eric just laughed.

"But I don't have keys to that!" Kat wailed.

"Who needs keys?" Eric put both hands on the hood and closed his eyes for a moment. The engine roared to life and everyone jumped. Everyone except Dylan. "Phil and I will tear up the road in this. They'll chase us, but I'll lose 'em and drive him far enough to get safely out of town. I'll probably have to change cars somewhere—"

"You're going to take my dad's car in a high speed chase and then ditch it??"

"Kat, I'm going to take very good care of this beauty, I promise. He'll get it back, good as new."

"I don't believe this…"

"I don't believe you're sticking me with this minivan," Dylan groaned and Eric laughed.

"Who says you're driving my mom's car?"

I guess I could see how this would be upsetting to Kat, but her priorities were confusing to me. I'd just ripped out all her kitchen cabinets, but *this* is what she was worrying about. "If Eric's taking Phil, that leaves Dylan as the first runner-up delinquent to drive the second getaway car, ok?"

"Sweet!" Eric exclaimed, slapping his hands down on the hood of the van and working his mojo to get it started.

"That's great. Now we can all die of carbon monoxide poisoning. And who are you calling a delinquent?" Dylan asked me.

"I wish I knew what was on the other side of that door. I'd hate to back up into anything when I go tearing out of here," Eric said.

Kat put her arms over her head.

"Um, I can help with that." Jessica walked to the garage door and put her hand on it. It disappeared.

We all jumped back.

"Don't worry. It…looks the same from out there—as it did before."

"Ok, Jessica. That's…awesome. Thank you," I said, wondering if there were anyone here who had the least little sense of discretion about using their Talent in front of others. Maybe this was some big "We Are Family" moment for some of them, but I wasn't feeling it. As soon as the thought went through my head I automatically looked over at Heather who pretended to be ignoring me. Great. *You and I are so going to talk after this.*

"Yeah, thanks, Jessie!" Eric walked over to study the lay of the land. I couldn't help but stare for a moment myself. I could still sort of see the outlines of the door, the horizontal lines of the panels, and the whole thing was kind of blurry. That, and the classical music coming out of the 'Vette, made me feel like I was in a movie.

From beyond where we could see, something came flying right at us. We all ducked, but of course whatever it was bounced off the door and onto the pavement.

"Gas!" Eric yelled, and then we all saw the smoke coming out of the canister, two more hitting the ground and smoke starting to curl up under the invisible door.

CHAPTER 12

Joss

"Just anywhere back in here is good. They won't be able to see us from the road, if anyone's looking."

Dylan pulled the van up onto the lawn where I said. He had to leave the engine running because, well, we didn't know how to turn it off. But at least it was quiet. We were at the rest area on the interstate, off the service drive and behind a hill. It was one of my family's emergency rendezvous points and the place I thought of automatically as a place for us to hide out and regroup.

The enormity of what had happened was trying really hard to get to me, and I was trying really hard to ignore it. My head was pounding and I kept seeing all the things I had done, all the ways I had used my abilities—in front of all these kids. In front of government agents! It was all sort of a blur now, and I was so tired I felt like I could curl up and go to sleep and convince myself it had been a nightmare—except for the smell of tear gas in my hair. We had all piled into the van, and I made Dylan wait to pull out until we saw Eric lead the agents away from the house. The gas had started to seep inside. Good luck getting that out of the upholstery.

Dylan tugged at my sleeve.

"Come on. Let's get some fresh air."

We all piled out, some of the kids dropping onto the grass just a few steps from the van, faking nonchalance and failing badly. I wasn't the only one who was damned shaken up from the evening's events—I didn't have to be psychic to know that. Speaking of which…

"How are you doing?" Dylan asked. "You don't look so good."

A) Aren't you the charmer, and b) Stop paying attention to me, it's freaking me out!!

He shrugged out of his jacket and was slipping it onto me before I could think to refuse it, and only a moment before my teeth started to chatter. It wasn't even that cold, but I was exhausted, hurting, freaked out, and exposed in this stupid outfit I'd forgotten about. I couldn't do anything but stammer a thank you and take a step back to get myself some distance. Of course the heel of Kat's stupid shoe sunk into the ground, which I wasn't used to, I stumbled sideways, and Dylan was there to catch me.

That's when Heather stepped in. "Hey Joss, I really gotta…you know. Walk with me."

I shrugged at Dylan as I set off with Heather, like I was resigned to my girly duty to accompany my kind to the bathroom. When I'd never done any such thing in my life. And now I had to do it walking around in these stupid shoes. The heels were low—I couldn't have walked in high ones—but they were pointy, and kept sinking. The things didn't even have toes. On top of everything else, I had cold feet. I was starting to get irritable.

"Ok, spill. How long have you been in my head? What do you know about me? Who have—"

"Before you ask me something that's just going to be really insulting, I'll just tell you, ok? I'm not in your head. Your head, his head, practically every head in this town— you're all over the place. You're all constantly yelling out your thoughts at me. So if you're going to expect me to apologize for hearing your mind chatter for the last decade or so—and girl, you think a lot—you can just forget it."

Well, that stopped me. "Yeah, yeah, all right. I get it. Sorry." And I did get it. We were born this way, and it wasn't like we could just snap our fingers and turn off the Talent.

"You say sorry and you're still thinking you don't trust me."

"You see why I feel this is a problem?"

Heather just grinned at me. "If it makes you feel better, I usually try not to listen to you because I know how private you are. But sometimes I just can't help it."

There were probably a lot of fascinating tidbits I could ask her about, but I needed to stick to the important stuff. "What happened back there…what I did…do they know it was me?"

"The agents? No. They don't have the first clue what happened. It was all a blur to them. As for the other kids…they're wondering. They're going over it in their heads and trying to figure it out. Some of them think that the way you took charge, the way you kept your head—they think that was your Talent, and someone else must have rearranged the furniture."

"And all these kids…are they all Talents?"

Heather thought for a moment. "Yeah, ok, I can't tell you that. It's not 'cause I don't know who is and who isn't. There are very few people I don't hear, but I don't think I can tell you something like that. It's not that I don't trust you, Joss," she added quickly. "I know who you are, what your principles are, and that you're probably about the most trustworthy person I know. But I have my own rules and I need to stick by them."

I supposed that, given how much Heather knew about how many people, that pretty much made my trustworthiness epic. But if that wasn't going to get me a pass on her rules—which I had to respect her for…

"What I *can* tell you," she continued, and I was kind of embarrassed knowing she was hearing what I was saying and what I wasn't, "is that the reason there are a bunch of Talents with us right now, is because there's a feeling of kinship among them. You felt it when everything started to go crazy—that's why you knocked the Taser out of that agent's hand. That's why, when you started barricading us in, Jessica joined us instead of slipping out the door. I think we all want to hang out with people who are like us, you know? Well, not you, but most people—and I get why you're like that. I mean, with Emily and all. But actually, even you *want*—"

"Things are going to go better between us if you don't do things like analyze my memories and tell me what I really want, 'k?"

"Yeah. Sorry. I knew that. Well, what I was saying was that the desire to find other Talents and sort of, I don't know, bond and band together…that's just out there. It's *been* out there. Everyone needs people to share their secrets with. But right now, with this group, it's more. It's like they've had a taste of their own power—"

"Oh God," I groaned.

"No, it's not like that. I mean that they saw how we could all stand together to protect one of our own. I mean, Joss, we totally *saved* Phil. From *NIAC*. We saved one of our own from our own personal boogeyman squad. Not everyone is clear that that's what they're feeling, but that's the gist of it. They want to organize, they need the security of that. And they want someone to take charge. They want—"

"Don't even."

"—you. I know, you don't want any part of a group anything. The very idea scares the crap out of you. It totally goes against your training and just your whole personality. And then, in a way, it totally doesn't. It's kind of also like totally who you are—inside. It's like your destiny."

This bit of insanity effectively rendered me speechless. I just turned and started walking back. I had pretty much caught on to the fact that my spoken responses were not really necessary—nor necessarily wanted.

"That's not true," she said, tagging along behind me. "Of course I want to hear what you choose to say. But also, I have to say that what you just thought about me was really not very nice." She threw up her hands when I turned to glare at her. "Not that I'm the thought police or anything."

We were nearly back to the others when I saw a pair of headlights coming around the bend.

"Ouch. Speaking of the thought police, here comes your dad. And, um, he's kind of pissed at you."

I wondered if telling me my dad's thoughts really fit in with Heather's avowed principles, but then, as soon as he got out of the car, it was pretty obvious. And it was obvious just by being obvious, if that makes any sense. Because Dad wouldn't show that anything was wrong if he could possibly help it. I could tell he was way agitated by the way he had swung around drive, pulled the car in front of the van and braked hard, leaving the back end half in the road and the lights on. He got out and started scanning the kids nearby, looking for me. I'd say I felt about half guilty about what I had caused, and half dread at having to deal with it.

I cringed some more when Dylan walked up to him. They were caught in the lights of the van and we had been sticking to the shadows, so even though Dylan gestured in the direction we had walked, I was pretty sure they couldn't see us yet. When Dad started to turn, Dylan quickly moved into his path and said something else. Dad became visibly belligerent, and I picked up my pace.

"I wish I could tell you what they're saying." Heather said in response to my thoughts.

I didn't bother to answer. And what was up with Dylan? His behavior was bordering on bizarre. He'd paid more attention to me in the last few hours than in the last ten years put together. Maybe I should have liked it, but…

"I wish I—"

"Yeah, yeah. Save it, Principle Girl."

I saw Dad catch sight of us, and I waved for good measure. He brushed Dylan off and started toward us.

"Jocelyn, what the hell are you involved in, young lady? Do you have any idea what's going on over the police band right now? The scanner's been non-stop with tales of your exploits—er, your friends'…"

"I know, Dad. I'm really sorry. Wrong place, wrong time," I said quickly, covering. Dad would have known my work when he heard about it, but for him to actually attribute it to me in front of others…This was really bad. "I tried not to get mixed up in it, but everything happened so fast. Can you take me home now, so I can tell you what happened?"

He swallowed hard, looking around us with jerky movements. He looked scared as well as angry, and my heart squeezed. I took his arm and started to steer him back toward the vehicles.

"Joss, hang on."

Dylan had snagged my hand, stopping me in my tracks. Not because he had grabbed on hard, but because he was touching me, and I couldn't make myself pull my fingers out of his light grasp if I'd wanted to. Which, apparently, I didn't. And knowing that Heather knew all that just added a layer of mortification. I managed to look up at him anyway.

"Are you sure you're going to be ok?"

For the blink of an eye, I wasn't sure what he meant, and then his eyes flicked over my shoulder to my dad and back to me. In that instant I was pissed enough on Dad's behalf to pull my hand away. I shrugged out of his jacket and held it out. "Of course," I said, with enough sting that I think he actually flinched. Of course I instantly regretted it, but I wasn't in any position to try to figure out what he might have meant or try to smooth things over. I wasn't even sure I should.

I wasn't sure of anything except that I wanted to lie down in the quiet for a while, and before that happened I had a lot of explaining to do.

Then Kat ran up, with Maddy and Elizabeth in tow. "Joss, you're leaving? Well, thanks for—" Kat stumbled, and she was looking over my shoulder. I imagined Heather was back there making some kind of sign to stop her from saying something stupid and getting me in more trouble. She gave this nervous little laugh. "I was going to say thanks for coming to my party, but I realized how stupid that was."

Dad tugged at me, and I started walking away. "Um, I guess I'll see you guys at school."

"I'll call you!" Kat waved.

As soon as we got in the car Dad said, "No phone. No visitors. You're coming right home after school every day. It's school and the store for you, from now on. I *knew* this party thing was a bad idea."

"I'm grounded?" It was a strange thing for me to have said, because what he was describing was just life as usual. I'd been grounded since age 5.

"You'll see it that way if you want to, but I'm just doing what I need to do to keep this family together. Some day you'll understand that."

Now that we were in the car and headed home, he seemed a bit calmer already.

"I understand it now, Dad, and you were right. It was a bad idea. Things got out of hand *so* fast."

"I went by the Dawsons' place first. Mr. Dawson brought me inside, past the *police line*," I cringed appropriately at the way he said it, "and I saw what you'd done. They're getting pictures of every bit of it, and they're talking about tracking down more witnesses for statements."

"I didn't do all of it," I said meekly. So then I proceeded to give him a play-by-play of events, trying to downplay as much as possible. But it was hard. I had to leave out the whole thing about Heather wanting me to make decisions because of what she saw in my head, because that would have sent Dad right over the edge. So I tried to make like I was just trapped with the group and following along.

Until I got to the part where we made our escape, at which point I think I was a little too into the story, and too into describing the way Eric peeled out of the garage backward as soon as the door would let the little car through, how he swung it around without even slowing down and without hitting the cars that were parked in the driveway, and then sped off across two lawns before hitting the street and disappearing.

"And then you drove everyone to the rest stop."

"Well, Dylan drove."

"Joss, you directed those kids to one of our family's safe zones, which has now been compromised."

I opened my mouth to respond, but didn't. He was right. I had done that. I had been trained about what to do in an emergency, how to keep thinking, how to assess options, and to have places in mind in case I needed them. I needed a safe place to take my group and so I used one of them. So yeah, the Marshall family had one less secret meet-up point, but didn't I count as a Marshall? Wasn't the point of it to be there in case any of us needed it? I found myself getting angry and chose not to answer while I calmed down.

"That Maxwell boy sniffing around you?"

"Dad! No! I mean…no. It's not like that."

"Good. I don't like him. You just steer clear of his type."

I pondered whether "his type" meant "cute boys," "all boys," or "humans," but kept my mouth shut. And then I pondered Dylan some more, and what was his deal tonight? I'd gotten pissed because I thought he'd insinuated that I might not be safe with my own father—who would tear lesser men in half to protect me, I knew. Dad's whole life was about protecting me, after all. But when I thought about it, what it might look like to someone else who didn't know him, well…maybe it was kind of ok that Dylan was concerned.

Or maybe it just violated all known Laws of the Universe.

CHAPTER 13

Joss

Grounded or not, when Sunday afternoon came around both my parents needed to be in the shop for an on-going sale, and someone had to take Jill to a birthday party in the park. Dad tried putting his foot down and grounding Jill too, but as she never really took to that like I did, she just cried until she turned purple. Mom suggested that I go to the store with Dad and she would do the party, but Dad didn't want me anywhere near the store with all those shopping cops. So, having promised soulfully that I would lead a blameless life evermore, I found myself sitting under a tree, a respectful distance away from the scary, second-grade set, waiting for Jill. The party had broken up, but she was still playing with a few other stragglers, and I wasn't in any mood to go home anyway.

"I'm sorry about the other night. What I said."

I jumped and stifled a shriek. Dylan was suddenly sitting next to me, like he'd just materialized out of the air—or out of my brain. How out of it was I that I never even saw him come up?

"I didn't mean to startle you. I just thought if you saw me coming you might leave."

"I'm waiting for my sister."

"Oh."

There was an awkward silence, so I thought about what he said.

"I'm not mad at you. The whole night was…messed up."

"Yeah."

Another silence.

"Kat tried to call you. Your mom says you're 'not available.' Grounded?"

"I guess."

"Sucks."

"I guess." *Duh. Come on, idiot. Say something.* "What happened after I left?"

"I drove everyone home, then Kat and I drove by her house, but it was still crazy over there, so we were driving down to the river to just kill some time when we saw Eric, so we picked him up. That was cool because it solved the problem of not having keys for the van. But then Eric said we should wipe the prints and leave it down there by the river in case someone wanted to say we stole it, so we ended up walking her all the way back home, and then the two of us went home."

"Sounds fun." I sounded sarcastic, but I think I meant it.

"Yeah, it wasn't the greatest night ever. What about you? Your dad seemed...I guess he was mad?"

"He was more freaked out than anything else. He's pretty over-protective, I guess, and that was the first party I'd been to since Emily Gianni's when I was five, so..."

"Hey, I think I went to that party. Scary-ass clown, right?"

"Yeah, there was. I don't remember much about it. I didn't remember you being there."

"My mom worked with her mom. I think possibly there was some kind of arranged marriage between me and Emily, but—well, whatever."

I didn't say anything.

"She was the first kid I knew of who got...taken. I remember my parents talking about it a lot—that was before they got divorced. They talked about whether or not they should try to explain it to me, or just not mention it, or what. My dad said if they didn't mention it then I'd just forget all about her, and I guess he won out."

"But you didn't. Forget her."

"I don't really remember her, so much as them fighting about her. How about you?"

"She was my best friend."

"Oh. Sorry. You know, I don't actually set out to say exactly the wrong thing every time I talk to you. It just comes naturally."

Ok, that actually made me crack a smile, and I was glad I wasn't facing him, so he didn't see it.

"Can I ask you something?" I said suddenly. "Why are you talking to me?" I hadn't planned on it, but I couldn't seem to stop myself.

"Um…I don't know if that's, like, a question I'm supposed to answer, or the kind of thing where I'm just supposed to apologize and walk away."

"I'm just asking. Because…I realize we don't run in the same circles or anything, but we've been in the same schools, in the same classes for, like, ever, and you've hardly said five words to me. And now it seems like all of a sudden you're talking to me every time I turn around." *Oh my God, could I be more abrasive? Maybe I could say it with Mace for a similar effect.*

"It just seems like that because you're a Joss." He bumped my shoulder with his, congenially. "This is a perfectly normal amount of talking. Trust me."

Why should I? I thought. I also thought I was being a bitch, but seriously, this was the Twilight Zone. Maybe he'd been body-snatched. Maybe…maybe Heather had given up her much vaunted principles to tell him I'd liked him forever. That was just the sort of thing Kat would think was just oh-so-cute. But then Dylan thought: oh great, freak girl likes me, but hey, may be good for laugh. So then he started talking to me and hinting that we're friends and stuff, just so he could lull me into a false sense of security so he could—

What? Come on, Joss. Really. Dial down the psycho. Does he really even think about you enough for that? Maybe he's just being nice.

I sighed and looked around, trying to get my bearings.

And saw Marco, crouched in the corner of the sandbox next to Jill, with roses blooming under her hands.

* * *

Dylan

Maybe we're not up to the teasing phase yet, I thought, judging by the scowl on Joss's profile. It seemed like I was always finding the wrong thing to say to her. It would've been fine with me to just sit there and not talk at all.

Suddenly, I felt her go completely rigid next to me. I leaned over to see what she was looking at.

Her little sister was in the sandbox, behind a small rose bush. It took me an instant to realize that it had no business being there, and that it was too perfect, too— unnatural. It was like a *Eureka!* moment. This, together with what Joss had said about Emily Gianni being her best friend, explained so much about why she was the way she was. And probably her dad too.

Joss's sister was a Talent.

All that was clicking into place in my head so fast that in that first moment I didn't even grasp the whole situation. But then Marco picked one of the roses, sniffed it, offered it to Jill, and looked right at Joss.

Son of a bitch.

"Son of a bitch!" Joss's hand cracked against my face so hard I had to catch myself with my hand to keep from falling over. "'Trust me.' Ugh! I am such an idiot! I should have known Marco would try something like this, and I should have known you'd be in it with him."

By the time I got to my feet, she was stomping across the sand and holding out her hand to her sister, who got up and went with her instantly. I tried to follow her, but Marco intercepted me by grabbing onto my arm. I knew there was no point in struggling if he didn't want to let me go yet.

"Ooh, that musta hurt, huh?"

"What are you doing with Joss's sister?"

"The kid was just showing me what she could do. Pretty cool, huh?"

"There's no way you can use something like that, so just leave her alone, ok?"

"If you say so, buddy. Now go on," he said, giving me a shove. "Make up with your girlfriend."

I sprinted over the hill, with my cheek still stinging, and the horrible sound of Joss's angry, agonized voice stuck in my head. They had stopped at the edge of the parking lot. Jill was sitting on the ground, with both legs wrapped around one of the wooden posts of the low fence that kept the cars off the grass, like she wasn't going anywhere. Joss was sitting on one of the cross pieces with her face in her hands. I had the terrifying idea that she was crying and thought about going invisible. But that was lame and wouldn't help, so I approached with caution.

She was saying, "I just don't understand how you could do such a thing. How many times have we told you, and told you—"

"But he's your friend. He said so."

"No! Marco is so not my friend. I—We don't have friends. Marshalls don't make friends. And this is why, Jill. This is what we've been trying to make you understand. Friends make you do stupid things."

"*He's* your friend. I 'member from the store."

Joss jerked her head up at that, and fixed me with a bright-eyed glare—she wasn't crying, but close. "No," she said, plenty loud enough for me to hear, "he's not. Let's go."

"Hey, just hang on." She was already on her feet, reaching for Jill, and I felt the need to grab onto her. But I didn't. "Calm down, Joss. You're making her cry."

"She damn well should be crying! You, of all people, understand exactly what she's done."

"What does that mean?"

"I wish you would stop playing dumb already. I know all about Marco and his blackmail. I was there when he gave his terms to Kat, remember? You were watching from across the lawn. I was there when she found the copies of the pictures of Krista in her locker."

"What pictures?"

"The ones of Krista using her Talent, that he used to turn her in when she wouldn't pay. And you know that, because you were probably there that day to check up and make sure that Kat had found them. I knew Jeff was in on it, because Marco made me watch Jeff harassing Trina. And I still can't figure out if that was to find out if she had a Talent or I did—which obviously neither of us does, but he still managed to get Kat to reveal herself."

"Wait, Kat has a Talent?"

"I swear, if you don't stop that, I'll hit you again."

I was starting to get really concerned about Joss. I was thinking about her dad, about the time he spent in the hospital, about how close to the edge he seemed to be. And now Joss was losing it. This was not the quiet, self-contained, never gets involved or opens her mouth girl I had been going to school with for years. And either she was suddenly spouting a lot of paranoid crazy talk, or there was a lot of shit going down, the guys I was calling my friends were shoveling it, and I had no clue it was happening. I wasn't really sure which was worse.

"I kept wanting to believe it was just something the two of them were doing, and you didn't know about it. Isn't it funny how stupid I am? Isn't it funny how I kept thinking how weird it was that you were talking to me, but kept telling myself to give you the benefit of the doubt, because you're such a nice guy? Why would I do that?"

"Because I *am* a nice guy!"

"You're a fucking extortionist."

"Joss, that's a bad word," Jill piped up.

"Shut up," she snapped back.

"Look, I don't know where all this is coming from, but I don't see how…I mean, look, Marco's a jerk. I *know* that. But you can't tell me he's been…" *Well, why not? He's using Joss's secret to make you rob a* bank, *for chrissake. He's got to be threatening to reveal Rob's secret, and how did he find that out in the first place? Jeff's jealous of Talents; he always has been…*

"What's the matter, Dylan? Run out of charm? Lies? That's ok, I was pretty much done listening anyway."

She yanked on Jill, who let herself be led, and they hurried off across the parking lot. I didn't even try to follow. I had some stuff to figure out.

CHAPTER 14

Joss

Monday morning it rained. Mom had dropped me off early because she had an appointment. I was hanging out in my spot thinking about how I needed to find a new place, and worrying that Marco would be coming up the stairs to hassle me any minute.

But instead it was Kat.

"Go away."

She just smiled, in that infuriating way she had while ignoring my wishes, and sat down next to me. "What's that about?"

"It's about go away, I want to be alone."

"You've been alone. I kept calling you all weekend but your parents wouldn't let me talk to you."

"Yeah, thanks, they really appreciated that."

"Well, they were being unreasonable."

"Did it ever occur to you that maybe I didn't—don't—want to talk to you?"

"Of course not. That would be insane. Anyway, look, I brought your stuff." She handed me a big bag with the clothes I'd left at her house.

"Thanks." I shrugged out of my second string jacket and dug my favorite one out of the bag. Then I went for the boots. I like what I like. "I didn't get your stuff washed yet."

"That's ok. I'm not hurting for clothes. So my mom's taking the day off work to stay home and wait for the insurance adjuster."

I cringed. "How's that gonna go?"

"I don't know, really. We'll just have to wait and see. We spent the rest of the weekend trying to clean up what

123

we could and eating all kinds of takeout. Damn, I can't believe what happened to my kitchen. Who do you think it was?"

She actually sounded like she thought the whole thing was cool. I shook my head. She was like an older version of Jill. I'd spent my weekend sick to my stomach and sleepless over what I'd done, what Jill had done, who would find out about it... And I don't think I could have faked enthusiasm for this conversation on a good day.

"Kat, would you please just leave me alone?"

"What's up with you?"

"What do you think is up with me?"

"I think you're cranky 'cause you got grounded. Which is totally bogus anyway. How was any of that your fault? I mean, if Phil had just kept his mouth shut...I'm *this close* to saying he deserved to get caught. And maybe we can also blame whoever started throwing Tasers—although that was totally cool, don't you think?"

"No, I don't think. Kat, *anything* could have happened. What if those guys had been using real bullets?"

"But they weren't. Maddy touched one of them, so she knew they weren't."

"What does that mean?"

"Didn't you wonder how she knew stuff? Or why she wears gloves all the time? Any time she touches someone, skin to skin, BAM! She knows everything about them. Everything they know, every thought they ever had."

"Jesus," I breathed, taking that in. *Note to self: stay AWAY from Maddy.* "Wait! Just stop." I put my hands over my ears. "I don't want to know this stuff."

"You already know this stuff. You were there. I'm just clarifying 'cause, you know, you're one of us."

"*What?!*"

"Part of our group, one of our friends, you know."

"No, I don't. I mean, I'm not. I don't want to be in your group. I don't want to be friends."

"What's up with that?"

"Just what I said. I don't want to be friends. With anyone. I just want to be left alone. Is that really so much to ask?"

"Girl, what is wrong with you? I have done everything I can think of to try to be nice to you, to bring you out of that shell of yours, and all you do is give me static. Did you have some kind of deeply scarring childhood trauma that makes you such a bitch?"

"My best friend was one of the first kids in Fairview who got taken to a State School. Because she burned a house down. One we were trapped inside. NIAC came and took her before we were even out of the hospital."

Kat just sat there with her mouth open. I could have gotten up and walked away at that point and she probably would have let me. But for some reason, my mouth just kept moving.

"We were five. It was summer. Emily lived next door to me, and we had played together since birth, practically. I always knew what she could do. But Trina was new and had just become our new bestest pal. We were the three Musketeers that summer, and we were going to let Trina in on the cool thing Emily could do." Actually, after Emily's demonstration, I was supposed to go next. But we never got that far, I had just about edited that part out of my head over the years, so I left that out.

"Trina? Jeff and Trina in the stairwell Trina?"

"Yeah, but this has *nothing* to do with that. So one day we left Emily's yard, snuck through the yard behind to the next street, and over to the house for sale two doors down. This was a huge adventure in itself. We got into the house and explored for a while, and then decided that the pink and purple bedroom of the girl who used to live there would be the place to show Trina the secret."

"So we gathered up some trash into the middle of the room, Emily held her hand over it, concentrated, and it burst into a little flame. It wasn't like it was the first time she had ever done something like that—or that I had seen it. But that time, there must have been something flammable on some of the trash because this flame just shot up in the air and burned her hand. She fell back screaming, and Trina and I were so busy trying to see her hand that we didn't notice the fire spreading and catching the curtains.

"It all happened so fast. It got so dark in there, and hard to breathe. We were just terrified little kids, so we couldn't think what to do or how to get out. We couldn't get the windows open to call for help or anything."

"That's horrible."

"It was horrible. We had gotten in through a window on the back porch, so we got back to the kitchen. But, I don't know, we got trapped in there somehow. I think part of the house collapsed because I remember that when the firemen got there, and heard us screaming, they had to come in with axes to get us out. They took us to the hospital, and as soon as we were stable, people started coming in and asking us how the fire had started.

"Emily and I knew that we were never supposed to say anything about what she could do, but Trina was new. She didn't know. And I think even if she had, her parents were really upset and telling her to tell the truth about how the fire started. So she did. And then Emily went away."

"Aw, honey, I'm really sorry."

"Yeah? Because I've spent all these years from then until now, trying to avoid having to go through anything like that again. And I was doing just fine until you came along. Then I had to start getting involved in your problems with Marco and look where that's gotten me. First the whole mess at your house, my parents are furious at me all over again, my dad's about to have a breakdown, and then my idiot little sister goes and reveals her Talent to Marco, of all people!"

"Wait. Wait, wait. Your sister's a Talent?"

I dropped my head into my hands. What the hell was wrong with me? "I can't believe I just said that."

"Joss, it's ok. You know I'm not going to tell anybody." She rubbed her hand in circles on my back and I actually wanted to lean into her. All this talking was making me crazy. So I told her, all about what happened at the park, about Jill and Marco. And I told her about Dylan, all my suspicions about how he kept talking to me, and then the fight we'd had...

"So wait, back up. You *hit* him?"

"Hard enough to knock teeth loose, maybe. I was pretty upset."

She actually laughed. "I'm sorry I missed that. But I don't really believe it."

"I don't believe I did it either, but I was pissed."

"No, I believe *that.* But not about Dylan. I don't think he'd do that."

"Why not?"

"I just don't. Hey! Let's ask Heather."

"Yeah, good luck with that."

"You're probably right. We'll get Maddy. I can talk her into it. Then you can know anything you want to."

I grabbed her arm, like I thought she was going to go do it right now. "No, don't do it. That's not right." There was still some stupid part of me that still wanted to believe Dylan might actually be innocent, and I hated the thought of someone violating his privacy like that. I'd spent part of my sleepless night imagining he would climb up to my window, prove his innocence, and tell me how he was going fix everything, get rid of Marco, save my sister, etc., and all because, he would confess, he had been in love with me from afar, lo these many years.

And I'd spent the rest of the night imagining all sorts of different ways to take him and his friends apart and hide the pieces.

Kat snorted. "And you mock Heather's rules. You're just as bad. Well, whatever. We'll figure it out. I totally screwed up that thing at my party—"

"I don't even want to talk about that."

"—but we'll come up with something. Don't worry, Joss."

Yeah, sure. I couldn't even manage to take on Kat and un-friend her. How was I supposed to fix my problems with Marco?

* * *

Joss

I waited on the lawn after school that day, waiting for Marco to approach me. I just wanted to know what he was going to ask for and get it over with. I had thought about going to lunch in the cafeteria again, so maybe he'd pass me a note or tell me when to meet him or something, but a) I didn't want to have to see Dylan sitting at his table—the liar, and b) I just couldn't deal with all those people. What had happened at Kat's party was all anyone was talking about, in ridiculous stage whispers, all day.

Anyway, there was nothing about the fact that I was waiting for Marco to come up to me, or pass me notes, that wasn't sick and wrong, and I spent my time alternating between fuming at Kat, Jill, and Dylan. Mostly Dylan.

"Sweetie, we have *got* to talk," Marco said, slinging his arm around my shoulders. I let him keep it there and steer me across the lawn, into the little courtyard where he and his friends like to duck out and smoke between classes. It reeked. I ducked out from under his arm and he let me, probably because there wouldn't be anyone to see us together anymore anyway. And if he wasn't humiliating me, what was the point?

"Just tell me what you want."

"You're so…direct. And I dig that about you, I really do. I want $500—"

"Ok, but it's going to take—"

"—a month."

"What?"

"But if you want to break that down into weekly installments, that's cool too."

"I can't pay you $500 a month, are you out of your mind? Where would I get that kind of money?"

"I'm sure your daddy would pay at least that much to keep your little sister's secret."

"I can't tell my dad about this. Besides, he would kill you."

"He might try. He just might. But he can't do anything to me from the locked ward at the loony bin, which is exactly where he'll be if he finds out about this, isn't it? After what happened at Kat's party while you were there, he's got to be right on the edge. What's it going to take to push him over?"

My mind went blank, like I couldn't process how Marco could know about my dad or the fact that he was threatening half my family now.

"So you don't want to ask your dad, but he's got that store, so… he's got stuff I like. I'm sure you can smuggle out enough in cash and prizes to keep me happy."

"I am *not* going to steal from my dad!"

"Since it's on your dad's behalf, I'd hardly call it stealing."

"You are out of your mind. I can't do that. Don't you think he's going to notice?"

"How is that my problem?"

"Look, I understand the position I'm in—"

"Do you?"

"—and I'm just asking that you be reasonable. Please."

It killed me to say it, but he really liked hearing it, if the grin spreading across his face was any indication. He swaggered over to me; that's the only way to describe it. His hand hit the wall next to my head and his body followed, but he stopped just short of falling against me.

"I think I can be reasonable. Since you 'understand your position' and all. I think I can be reasonable if you can. 'Cause you know that I've always liked you, Joss."

I started swearing a blue streak in my head, but I kept looking him in the eye. I couldn't show weakness now, even though I thought I could see where this was going, and I was terrified about what my answer would have to be.

He flicked the hair back off my shoulder, just a quick, light brush to see if he could touch me without me hauling off and knocking his teeth out. And I so wanted to. With some concentration on my part, the air between us would gather and focus and then blast him back into the bricks on the other side of the courtyard. But I had to hold it back. His hand settled on my cheek.

This is what Trina felt like when you didn't help her.

"You want me to be your girlfriend," I guessed.

"Well…yes and no. See, I'm at a point in my life where I don't feel like I want to be tied down to one 'girlfriend' per se. But of course I am interested in female companionship from time to time, and I could be interested in your female companionship on a fairly regular basis, say—"

"You piece of shit!" Dylan just came in out of nowhere, shoving Marco back, away from me. "She's not gonna be your…"

"Whore, Dylan. The word is whore."

I grabbed onto Dylan's raised arm, putting all my weight into it and wishing, not for the first time, that I could control animate objects as well as inanimate ones. Then I could just make Marco walk off a bridge or something.

"Dylan, cut it out," I said. "This doesn't concern you."

CHAPTER 15

Dylan

Marco had a laugh at that.

"The two of you," he shook his head. "Doesn't it look like this concerns him?"

I really wanted to beat his face in, but it was stupid, me standing there, pretending like I could, and knowing I'd never walk away. I lowered my arm. I had the urge to draw Joss against me, put her behind me, make some kind of he-man statement that she was under my protection. But who was I kidding? Not either one of them.

"I mean, you've got no idea, Joss, what this guy's been willing to do to keep your dad's *issues* a secret. And now he's willing to go to the mat for you over a little name-calling, let alone the rest of what we were talking about."

"I wish you would shut the fuck up."

"You knew? About my dad?"

I turned to her, unsure of what to say or how she was going to react to that. I guess I should have told her I knew? Whatever I decided, it was always the wrong thing.

"Marco found out from someone at the hospital, a long time ago. He told me back then, and I thought he was going to keep it to himself. I'd pretty much forgotten about it until he brought it up last week."

"Why did he—?"

"Because I wanted something from Dylan, something that's not your business. Given his obvious interest in you lately, I thought it was time to pull that one out of my hat. Worked like a charm, too."

"But he's your friend."

Marco narrowed his eyes on me. "I thought that too. But I think we've been growing apart."

"I'd say so."

"But still, he's got his uses. Want to tell her how useful you are?"

"No."

"I think you're right about that. The less she knows, the better. Girls are so chatty. Take little Miss Jill, for example."

"Seriously, dude, leave her alone. She's just a little kid." I was wondering how much rage I could hold back before I just exploded. By the time I had left Joss the day before, Marco had disappeared. He was good at avoiding me when he wanted to, especially when he had Jeff to run interference for him, like he'd had all day today. So I hadn't even been able to confront him about Joss's accusations. Didn't need to now.

"Oh, I want to leave her alone. But I've got bills to pay."

"What is up with your obsessive need for cash lately?"

"That's none of your business!" Marco snapped, looking deadly. "You and I have a deal and part of it is that my business is my business."

"Take my share then."

"Your share of what?" Joss asked.

I ignored her. "I was getting a share, right? That's what you told us. I'll do what I said I'd do, you keep my share, and you leave Joss and her family alone."

"How do you know your share was worth that much?"

"Because you can't pull this off without—"

"Just…watch what you say."

I turned to Joss who was completely unreadable as usual. "Would you go home, please, so we can work this out?"

"No," she said indignantly, and maybe with an edge of concern? Or maybe that was just my imagination. "What are you doing? You can't—"

134

"Joss, please. Just go, ok?"

"Yeah, Joss. I'm intrigued by what Dylan thinks he has to bargain with, so you just run along home."

"Please," I added.

She looked from one of us to the other, shook her head. "Don't be stupid."

Too late for that, I thought as I watched her walk away. Then I turned back to negotiate with my ex-best-friend.

Satan.

* * *

Joss

What the hell?

That was really the thrust of my thoughts. They'd go off in one direction, and then off in another, but that's the phrase I kept coming back to. I was seriously down the rabbit hole. Everything was going wrong, everything was crazy—

Speaking of crazy, my dad was the one who was supposed to pick up Jill today, and would be waiting at home for me. As soon as I thought that, I felt bad about it. My dad wasn't crazy, not really, he just got really stressed out, and then his reactions weren't exactly within the normal range. But hey, what about our family was normal anyway? The point was that dad was going to grill me about why I was late and I was afraid that I was too distracted by all the crazy to lie effectively. It was one of those rare times when I was wishing a friend would see me walking and stop by to give me a ride home.

And wasn't making friends what got me into this whole mess in the first place?

The blast of a car horn right next to me made me jump and a door swung open.

Okay, that's just weird.

Not just weird, though. It was also scary and irritating when I leaned down and saw Dobbs behind the wheel.

"Need a ride, Jocelyn?"

"Oh, no thanks, Mr. Dobbs. It's a pretty nice day. I was actually looking forward to the walk."

"Hmm. Well, look Joss, Marco Finelli came to see me this morning, and our conversation brought up a few questions I'd like to ask you. I thought maybe we could chat now, but if you'd rather, I could call your parents in and we could have a conference during school hours. I figured this way you wouldn't have to miss any class."

"Oh, well, that's a good idea," I said, getting into the car. What else could I do? "I don't really like missing class."

"Such a good student."

He pulled away from the curb and headed toward our neighborhood. The good news was that I didn't live too far away by car, so this couldn't go on too long. But still, I was going to be a lot more careful what I wished for from here out. Clearly the Universe was listening—with the sole purpose of smiting me for Its own amusement.

"Marco was kind enough to bring me some interesting photographs taken by the authorities after that rather upsetting episode at the Dawson home over the weekend."

"Really? How did he get those?"

"I really didn't ask, Jocelyn. I believe Marco has some...*connections*. Suffice it to say that he knows I take an interest in these sorts of...occurrences, if you will, and brought me copies of these photographs." He pulled a large, clasp envelope from between the seats. "Here, take a look."

Opening that envelope was about the last thing I wanted to do. The last time I'd seen an envelope of photos someone had received from Marco, they'd scared the crap out of me. But at the same time, there was no way I could refuse. I had to know.

The first picture wasn't even of Kat's house. I was sure of that. It was a black and white photo, a little grainy. The kitchen was much smaller, and seemed…dated. Although that was really hard to tell because every one of the cabinets was pulled from the walls. And yeah, that creeped me out. I could see where this was going, but still, something nagged at me about it. Like I should know this. And then I saw the charred wood at the edges of the scene.

"No, not that one," Dobbs interrupted my inner freak-out. "Look at the next one."

The other photo was my first glimpse of what I'd done to Kat's kitchen. Wow. I knew when I did it that it was bad, but…Wow. Just a few days ago I had been in that kitchen, that big, spacious, immaculately clean and modern kitchen, helping Kat get ready for the party. In the photo I held it looked like a wrecking crew had been in, stripped it down for a complete remodel, and just piled up the old stuff against a wall like so much garbage.

Only the wrecking crew had been just me.

Joss Marshall: Homewrecker.

"I find it interesting, how similar the two photos are, don't you? As soon as I saw this one, it just struck me as so familiar that I had to run home during my lunch hour and pull that other one off my home computer."

I shrugged. "It's two messed up kitchens."

"Doesn't that first one look familiar to you at all?"

"No, should it?"

"Well, I realize you were very young at the time, but that's the kitchen where the fire department found Emily Gianni, Trina Halston, and you."

"Oh," I said. I didn't really have a glib reply. I mean, I had kind of figured that out, but I was still trying to process it. I totally didn't remember doing any of that. But then, that whole thing was so jumbled in my mind. We were so scared, panicked—

"It's interesting, don't you think, the fact that you seem to be the common denominator in these two incidents?"

I shrugged. "I think it doesn't take much to qualify as interesting with you. But I guess that's nice for a guy like you, who doesn't get out too much. But then, neither do I," I added quickly, as though I hadn't meant anything by it. "What made you think I was there? At the party I mean."

"Marco. He was kind enough to give me information about who attended, including his recollection about who was inside the house at the time the agents were attacked, and names he's gathered from others after the fact. Naturally, when your name came up, it stood out for me, since we're neighbors and I've known you and your family for such a long time. I do take a special interest in you, you know. And look, here we are."

He pulled into his driveway and I hopped out of the car before he'd turned off the engine. I did not want to get trapped in there for one more minute.

"Well, thanks a lot for the ride."

"My pleasure, Jocelyn. Anytime."

I threw him a fake smile and started down the driveway.

"And Joss?"

Reluctantly, I turned around.

"Anytime you want to talk. You know I'm always watching out for you."

Don't I know it.

* * *

138

Dylan

I walked over to Joss's house feeling tired and sick, and wishing that dealing with Marco as an adversary didn't make me shake in my boots. If I wanted to be all self-analytical, I guess that's why I'd stayed friends with him for so long and made myself ignore what a jerk he was growing into. Because as long as I was his friend, I knew I was safe. From him and probably from anyone who'd want to mess with me.

I knew Rob hoped that I could get us out of the bank job, but he was just going to have to deal, like I was. Just like Kat was going to have to work her own stuff out. At least I could tell Joss that everything was taken care of where she was concerned, and that her family was safe, for now.

I walked up to the door and rang the bell. I thought I deserved to entertain a fantasy, as I stood there waiting, about her throwing herself into my arms in gratitude. But I was feeling too much like a beat-down loser to really get into it.

And because that's just how things were going, it wasn't Joss who answered, but her dad, and he did not look happy to see me.

"What do you want?"

"Uh, hi, Mr. Marshall. I…just dropped by…to talk to Joss. Is…she around?"

"She's not seeing anyone."

"Oh. Um, is she ok?" She was probably really upset when she left us. I thought it was clear that I was going to report back to her on what Marco and I talked about, but maybe she didn't mention that to her dad and locked herself in her room or something.

"She's fine. But she's not having any visitors."

"Oh. Ok. Well, maybe you could just tell her I stopped by and that I'll call her later?"

"No phone calls. My daughter doesn't need you, or any of your friends, getting her into trouble."

"Did she tell you that?"

"I'm telling you that!"

"Yes sir." *Damn, take my head off, too.* "Mr. Marshall, what happened at that party, that wasn't our fault. I mean, sure, there were some Talents there who got out of hand, but I think if you'd been there, you'd have to agree that they were—"

"Maxwell, I have zero interest in your analysis of last weekend's events. I know what happened and whose fault it was. And Jocelyn is clear that it's in her best interests not to have anything to do with the likes of you or any of that crowd. So you need to go and take your interest elsewhere. Are we clear, son?"

"Crystal. Sir."

"That's fine then."

Then he shut the door in my face.

I could feel him watching me as I shuffled back to the sidewalk and down the street. I really wanted to talk to Joss. I told myself that it was because I didn't want her to keep worrying about Marco demanding money or— anything else. I wasn't even going to think about what else he'd said to her because it still made my blood boil. Her dad was probably really stressing her out, since the party, and there was the whole thing with Jill that she was crazy upset over—with good reason. I could tell her tomorrow, but I just didn't think she should have to lose anymore sleep over Marco.

Plus, yeah, I just wanted to see her. That's why I didn't just call. And now, with what her dad said, I guess I kinda wanted to see if the fact that she was "clear" about her best interests meant that she actually agreed with him.

I walked up someone's driveway, between where their chimney stuck out from their house and where their giant SUV was parked, a place that afforded me as much cover as anywhere else I was going to find, and disappeared. Then I walked back to Joss's.

I had no idea where her room was in the house, or even if she would be in it. But there were a couple of good trees in the yard that looked sturdy and the little house had a wrap-around porch that meant most of the bedrooms would have windows over a gently sloped roof. Let's just say I had snuck into places that were more complicated than that.

I moved carefully, trying not to shake the tree any more than the wind would, trying to keep my footsteps light on the porch roof, testing my steps before I took them, looking for loose shingles. Because let's face it, slipping, bouncing off the roof, and falling to my doom was not the stealthy way to go.

When I found Joss's room, I wasn't surprised to find it pretty Spartan, and more neat because there just wasn't much to make a mess with, than neat with military precision. Joss was lying on her stomach, with her head on her crossed arms, and her face was turned away from me. I wondered if she was sleeping, but my toes were falling asleep from squatting down at the window, so I tapped on it.

She immediately bolted up in bed and I could see that she'd been crying. In a moment of panic, I thought about winking out again, but I didn't. I just kind of lamely waved at her through the window. She swiped at her face as she ran over, did something with a set of wires on the sill, and pushed the window up.

"What the hell are you doing here?"

CHAPTER 16

Joss

I honestly don't know what was worse, the shock of having Dylan crouched on my roof, the terror that my dad would come storming up the stairs at any moment and kill him, or the mortification that Dylan had caught me crying like a girl and looking more hag-like than usual.

"Did you know your dad said no phone calls and no visitors?" He gave me that crooked smile of his that usually made me go completely dumb, but right now was just too ridiculous. Did everyone in this town just love living on the edge?

I actually grabbed him by the front of his jacket and hauled him into the room. "What if someone sees you up there? What if they tell my dad? What if he comes up here and shoots you? Jesus."

That seemed to make him think. He cocked his head. "You really think he'd shoot me?"

"*I* might shoot you. What. Are. You. Doing here?"

"I came to tell you the rest of what happened with Marco. I guess I *kinda* thought you'd be interested."

"Well, yeah, I just didn't think—I'm sorry." I flopped down on the footlocker at the end of my bed, wiping my face again with a push my hair back gesture that I hoped wasn't too obvious. "You didn't have to go to so much trouble."

"Tree climbing is one of my specialties," he said, sitting next to me. I wondered if it looked like I left him room to sit there on purpose.

"I'll bet."

We were quiet for a moment, and we were alone, so I thought maybe it was best to just get this part over with.

"I'm sorry I hit you."

"Oh, yeah," he said, rubbing his cheek. "I forgot about that."

Boys. "And I'm sorry I accused you of being in on Marco's blackmail thing, and trying to distract me so he could trick my sister, and whatever other nasty thing I said to you. Clearly, I was wrong."

"Yeah, well, that's okay. I guess it looked pretty bad from your perspective."

From my perspective, I still can't figure out what's going on. You being subhuman slime in league with Marco makes more sense than you being here, in my room.

"I've been a complete idiot where Marco's concerned. I should have cut ties with him a long time ago, but I..."

"You don't have to explain anything to me."

"It's complicated."

"Okay." I tried to let it be okay, but it really wasn't. I really wanted to understand what was going on with him. "What you said at Kat's party, about Marco..."

"What did I say?"

"You said he makes you do things you didn't think you'd do, or something like that. Was that about the thing with my dad? What Marco's making you do to keep quiet about that?"

"Joss...What I came by to tell you is that you don't need to worry about that, okay? Marco's not going to say anything to anyone about your dad or Jill."

"Because of what you're doing for him. What is it? I know he doesn't want you to tell me—"

"Fuck him. Excuse me."

"—but I want to know."

Dylan sighed. "It's not that I don't want to tell you because Marco said so, it's just..." He shook his head. "Okay, you might as well know what a miscreant I've been. Marco and I, and Jeff and now Eric...we...." He made a frustrated noise and then pushed on quickly, "We're criminals. We vandalize, we joyride, and mostly we steal stuff, some of which we play around with and then throw away, some we fence for cash… It sounds bad—it is bad. I know it is. It just seemed like it was little stuff, you know? No big deal."

So Dylan was reluctant to tell me about his petty crime career, why? Because he didn't want me to think badly of him? Or maybe he was just ashamed of himself. Which he should be. As the daughter of an independent merchant, it was kind of hard not to be pissed off at that attitude.

"No big deal," I repeated, making sure there was some judgment in my tone. "But it doesn't seem like that anymore?"

"No, not anymore."

"What's he making you do?"

"Rob a bank."

"Rob a—" I jumped up, totally forgetting where we were. Dylan caught my hand, his eyes going wide, and I clamped my other hand over my mouth. He pulled me back down next to him, but he didn't look at me.

"It's just a grocery store bank."

"Oh well, if that's all…" I snarked.

"Yeah, I know.

"Then, yeah, do they have an it's-only-a-grocery-store-bank-larceny charge?"

"I know, okay?"

Oh, I was such a bitch. Whose crazy family was the reason Dylan was becoming a bank robber? Yep. Mine. And I was giving him a hard time about it. But why shouldn't I? This was the dumbest thing I'd ever heard.

"You cannot do that. You just can't. And not for me. That's just stupid."

"Joss…"

"I said no."

He laughed a little. "You are so not the boss of me."

"Dylan, seriously. Please. Don't do that. I'll talk to Marco again and we can—" He stiffened next to me and I remembered the way he'd looked when he'd come in swinging at Marco. Maybe best not to stay on that subject. "I'll figure something out."

"It's practically done already. It's not a crazy plan, either. There are some other Talents involved, besides Marco. I actually think it's going to work. And it's not like I've never committed a crime before, so there's no reason for you to worry about my immortal soul or anything. Just…let it go."

I went over what he said in my head a few times, and kept hearing the same thing.

"Did you just say Marco is a Talent?"

"Yeah, has that not been covered yet?"

"Um, no."

"That's pretty much the only reason I had a hard time believing what you said about him blackmailing Talents. It's just too many kinds of messed up, you know? Even for him."

"Yeah." Yeah, it was messed up. But too messed up for Marco? No, not really. "So…what can he do?"

"He's strong. Like pick up a truck and hold it over his head strong."

"Oh." I thought about Dylan growing up with a best friend who could easily kill him if he ever got ticked off. It kind of explained a lot about how Dylan was always trying to be charming and likable, and smoothing things over. And I thought about how I had held him back from throwing the first punch today. *Idiot.*

"You know, there's a lot of stuff I'm not proud of. Seems like the more I think about stuff I've done, how I've acted, the more there is."

I wasn't sure I was up to hearing any more of Dylan's true confessions. Part of me wanted him to keep talking, was eager to hear any scrap he wanted to reveal about himself, good or bad. But a voice in the back of my mind was freaking out about what it seemed Dylan was willing to do for me. *Me.* And I was also scared about the sense of connection I was feeling, the urge to reach out and take his hand. I needed to bring us back to the subject at hand.

"So the grocery store thing, that's it, right? You and Marco are done, even, it's all over?"

"Yeah," he said, but he'd hesitated.

I punched him in the arm, pretty hard. "You. Are a lousy liar, do you know that?"

"Ow, and volume, and I know now, okay? Geez." He rubbed his arm.

"Don't be a baby." Part of me couldn't believe I was feeling this comfortable with him right now. "What else?"

"One more thing."

"What?"

"I don't know. I just had to agree that when he needed me again, I would do one more thing for him."

"And if it's Murder One?"

"It's not going to be Murder One."

I ignored him. "And then that's not going to be enough, you still won't be even. Then it's going to be just one more thing, and one more after that, and you are never going to get away from him." Just like Dobbs was never going to stop, just like Jill was never going to be trustworthy, especially when she had people like Dylan to pay the price for her mistakes, just like Dad was never going to be stable. Someday, something was going to get back to him and send him back to the hospital—or worse. None of it was ever going to stop, ever.

To my horror, a sob rose up in my throat, and I slapped my hand over my mouth to keep it in. But then there was another one right behind it. My mind was in that same loop it had been in before Dylan showed up, only now with more information.

"Hey," he said gently, his arm wrapping around my shoulders. "You don't have to cry about it."

Somehow, though, that just made it worse, and I really did have to cry about it. It was horrible, and trying not to only seemed to make it worse. My shoulders started to shake as I tried to just be quiet about it. What if Dad heard me? I should get Dylan back out the window right now.

He turned toward me, pulling me in so my head rested on his shoulder. And instead of pushing him away, I latched onto his jacket and cried harder. Which was stupid because he was so warm and he felt *really* good. I never cried; I never even let anyone know I was upset, and this was just so wrong. But in a rational world, Dylan shouldn't even be talking to me, let alone sneaking into my room or promising to commit grand larceny on my behalf. And it was partly that overwhelming sense of unreality that was making me crazy. How was I ever going to get all this impossible stuff worked out if the Laws of the Universe kept changing all the time?

I was never going to get anything worked out. Ever.

When I pushed away from Dylan, he didn't try to hold on to me. I retreated to the table beside my bed for a handful of tissues to mop my face. I felt more than heard him come up behind me, and then he put his hands on my shoulders.

"It's ok, you know."

"Sure."

"If it makes you feel any better, your dad almost made me cry earlier."

I snorted. "It really doesn't."

"Sorry."

I could easily have leaned back against him. I wondered what he'd think of that, or what he'd do. I wondered what was going on between us.

"Is there something else you're not telling me?"

"Mr. Dobbs drove me home today." Now why did I say that?

"Mr. Dobbs the guidance counselor?"

And then I was pouring out another story to him, with background details and everything, about how Dobbs was always harassing me, like he was trying to get me to slip up and say something.

"About your sister."

"Yeah, I guess," I lied automatically.

"And these pictures…"

"He thinks that because I was there for both incidents, that I must have had something to do with it. And even if he can't prove it, I can't have that kind of attention directed towards me. Not with my family stuff."

"Yeah, I see what you're saying. So what are you going to do?"

"I don't know what I *can* do. Just keep doing what I've been doing, denying, deflecting. I guess it's not such a big deal. I just hate that guy and it's just one more thing."

"I'll get the pictures."

"What?"

"I'll get the pictures."

"How?"

"I'll go to his house, get the pictures."

"Are you out of your mind?"

"I steal stuff. It's one of my specialties."

I dropped my head into my hands.

"It's stupid, Dylan. He's probably got copies on his computer—"

"That's ok. I know a guy."

"So you propose to involve more people in crime on my account?" I turned to face him, but he was already backing away toward the window.

"I'm not proposing anything. I'm just doing."

"No."

"Did I mention how you're not the boss of me?" he grinned.

* * *

Dylan

"Just put your foot here, then, when you can reach that limb, grab it. Didn't you ever climb a tree before?"

"Unlike you and your friends, this life of crime is new to me. And not my choice, I'll remind you." Rob pushed his glasses up and put his foot in my hands. "Why am I doing this again?"

"Because I asked you to and I'm the guy who's covering your bacon on Thursday. So you're happy to do me this favor."

Rob grunted as he pulled himself up onto the branch. A few well-placed steps and he was over the fence and wrapped around the tree trunk looking down. I vaulted up, using the fence, swung into the tree, and dropped down into Dobbs' yard.

"And I thought you were the cool one."

"I *am* the cool one." And then I just felt bad. "Look, if this is such a big problem for you, then just tell me how to find what I'm looking for and go home."

"Yeah, 'cause it's that simple." He dropped down next to me. "Lead on."

I started across the yard toward the house, but I had only taken a few steps when he grabbed the back of my jacket and hauled me back. "Vanish," he hissed.

I did, and Rob moved me around like a picket sign until he was satisfied.

"Look up there. At the edge of the house. See that red light? That's a camera. Who's got camera surveillance for their front yard?"

"Mr. Dobbs, apparently."

"Who's Mr.—Mr. Dobbs, the guidance counselor? What the hell are we doing here?"

"I heard they caught you chewing gum in the library, so we're here to erase it from your permanent record so you can still get into Harvard."

Rob punched me. "MIT, you moron. Let's just get it over with, whatever it is."

Mr. Dobbs had a big, older house with a basement, and I had decided that one of the basement windows was the way to go. Just as I'd hoped, it wasn't hard to force one enough to squeeze through and drop down into the house.

We found Dobbs's computer in a home-office type area he'd set up in what was supposed to be the dining room. I started rummaging in the desk while Rob went at the computer. I hadn't seen him do his thing before, and I'll admit I kind of forgot what I was doing while I watched. He didn't fumble for the power switch and wait for it to boot up. He just put his hand on the box and lights came on, stuff started whirring inside, and stuff started flashing across the screen.

"How can you read that?" I whispered.

"Not. Reading."

It sounded like talking was difficult for him, so I shrugged and went back to the drawers. I found the pictures Joss was talking about, and I could see the similarities in the two scenes. I had wondered who had been doing the heavy lifting at Kat's house. Since Sunday, I'd had it fixed in my mind that Jill having a Talent explained a lot about Joss. But if Joss had a Talent…

151

That was some serious power. Was it seriously wrong how completely hot I thought that was?

Rob snapped his fingers in front of my face. "Maxwell, wake up! Check this out." He was holding his hand out flat, about an inch over the computer, and there was this faint, pale light in the space between. "On the screen, moron."

To be honest, there were just a lot of words on the screen, and some graphics, and I had a lot in my head right then. "Could you just...sum it up?"

Rob looked at me like he was concerned I couldn't read. "Fine. It basically indicates that Mr. Dobbs, the mild-mannered guidance counselor we all know and love, is...a NIAC agent. The two paychecks kind of explains the size of this house, come to think of it."

"Wait, wait, what now?"

"It would be *quieter* if you could read it *yourself?* These are emails," there was some slight movement of his hand, and the words began to scroll, "weekly reports from Dobbs to NIAC with interviews he's conducted, observations, and basically anything he finds suspicious with his intentions to follow up on it."

I started cussing.

"Is that really necessary right now? I think he's making some of this stuff up, just to show he's doing stuff and make himself seem more important, to be honest." For some reason, Rob didn't seem very concerned. He must not have found his name in an email yet.

"Ok, so Dobbs is NIAC. What else is there?" Because sneaking into an annoying guidance counselor's house was one thing, but this was something else, and I was getting nervous. Rob seemed to be fine as long as he was communing with the machine.

"There are some files here." He read off some names, a bunch of which were kids I knew, but no one from our crew. They could be Talents, or it could be bullshit. Curiosity was getting the better of me. I wondered if Rob could copy the files.

"Open Joss's but don't look at it."

"I can't."

"What do you mean you can't?"

"I can't show it to you without looking at it. All this stuff we're looking at's encrypted. I'm translating it as we go."

"How do you do that?" He looked at me like: *how the hell should I know? How do you disappear? Touché.* "Ok, fine, but ponder your slow and painful death if I think you've talked about any of this."

"Is *this* why we're here? Because Dobbs has dirt on your girlfriend?"

"She's not my—never mind."

"I think that's nice."

"What's in the damned file?"

"Not much. Mostly speculation about some fire…Oh yeah, I remember that. Huh."

I read it over his shoulder. He was right. There wasn't much there. Still, he'd documented a ton of meetings with Joss and details about how he'd grilled her and what her responses were. I would have loved to have choked him with one of his ridiculous Looney Tunes neckties just then.

"Get rid of it. All of it. You can do that, right? Get rid of all the Talent files?"

"Well, yeah, but…"

"Then do it!"

"Look, I can't just go in and excise the Talent files and not touch anything else. It would be too obvious that someone came in and did something."

"It's going to be just as obvious if I have to throw the thing out the window. Only louder."

"Hang on, hang on. I didn't know you were so hot-headed. I can take care of this, make it look like a malfunction or a virus caused massive and irretrievable data loss."

"Fine. Do that."

"But we don't know if there are copies. We don't know if this stuff has already gone to NIAC."

"And if we did know that, what would we do about it? We've been here too long already, but we've found out more than we came for. So let's just take what we have and get lost. 'K?"

"Yeah. Fair enough."

While Rob took a few more minutes to do his thing, I finished going through the desk. I found a few more envelopes with photos, but they didn't have anything to do with Joss, me, or Rob. I felt bad leaving them there, but one envelope he could write off as misplaced and hopefully go crazy looking for it. If all of them went missing, he would definitely know we'd been there.

"That's it!" Rob said as everything shut down. "Please let's get out of here."

That was more than cool with me. We thought it was best to go back out the way we'd come in, even though getting up through the window was a little tricky for Rob. I ended up standing him on my shoulders and practically launching him through.

Finally, we were off the property. Joss's pictures were stiff in my jacket, and I thought about going across the street, climbing up to her window, and presenting them to her. But we had already been incredibly lucky, and NIAC agent or not, I was more scared of Mr. Marshall than Mr. Dobbs. Plus, I had dragged Rob along on this, and it turned out I'd needed his help more than I'd thought I would. The least I could do was walk home with him.

It's a good thing I did, too, because getting him back into the house and back in his room was where we ran into trouble. Not too bad, though. I just had to cover him as his mom walked by on her way back from raiding the kitchen.

"Thanks," Rob whispered. "Um, sorry about that."

"No problem. I…didn't look." Sometimes when you're invisible, you see things that are really embarrassing.

"Well, we're brothers for life now."

I have to say that I really liked Rob. "Life or longer. Look, thanks a lot for coming with me tonight. I was in way over my head and I really needed your help. I owe you."

"Yeah, well, just keep me out of jail."

"I got your back."

I turned to open the window, but he stopped me.

"Dylan, there's something else I've gotta tell you. Something I found in the computer…"

CHAPTER 17

Joss

I inadvertently had lunch with Dylan on Tuesday. He was the latest invader of my stairwell space. I blame Kat.

He led with the pictures and didn't give me a chance to feel too awkward about my meltdown the day before, nor did he let me coo over how he got them for me. Which was cool, because I'm not the cooing type. Instead he launched into a rapid info-dump. I was trying to get over the fact that he got poor Rob involved in my problems, and in breaking and entering. Plus, it's not always easy for me to think when Dylan's talking to me. So I really didn't get a chance to start processing it until History.

Mr. Dobbs was working for NIAC. With encrypted files on us and everything. It made him seem like more, somehow. Not just an obnoxious loser who wanted to build himself up by destroying our lives, but now an obnoxious loser who wanted to build himself up by destroying our lives who had a badge. I mean probably, somewhere, he'd have a badge, right?

Anyway, bottom line: more to hate, more to be worried about. Just what I needed. And Dylan said there was a narc. NIAC had planted someone among us, someone we thought was a student, and they were sending information back to NIAC. Who? Could be anyone. Was it Marco?

I'd been up all night thinking about what to do about him, and I thought I was close to coming up with something that might just save Jill, Kat, and even Dylan—all of us. But if Marco was already known to NIAC, it wasn't going to work. How the hell was I going to find that out, just ask him?

I leaned back in my seat and let my gaze wander the room. Maybe if I sort of emptied out my head and started over fresh it would look different. And then I noticed Heather sitting over by the windows. She was looking at the teacher, but she wasn't taking any notes. Her pencil was vertical and she was lifting and dropping it, bouncing it on its eraser.

Heather. Are you tuned to Joss network? Tap your pencil, once for yes, twice for no.

Tap. She turned and looked at me sheepishly.

Ok, don't worry about that, and don't look at me. Did you get all that stuff about Dobbs being affiliated with NIAC?

Tap. And she gave me this wide-eyed *eeep!* sort of look.

Seriously, face front, okay? Did you hear what I thought about the narc? Do you know who it is?

Two taps for that one. Of course, that would be too easy. Then I had another thought.

Would you tell me if you did?

Tap.

Can you tell me if it's Marco?

Tap.

Damn. That bastard.

Tap tap.

What, he's not a bastard? Ok, wait. Syntax. Is Marco working for NIAC undercover?

Tap tap.

So it's not Marco. Ok. Then all we have to do is get you to listen in on everyone in the school until you find out who it is.

Tap tap.

I'm sure it's a pain and against your rules, but this is really important.

Tap tap.

No, what? Oh my God, this is so annoying.

"Jocelyn. Are you with us? Do you have any thoughts on this question?" Mr. Grier asked, rather snidely. I guess I'd been too obviously not paying attention. Crap.

I felt a hand on my back and then words, and the desire to say them, just popped into my head. "Um, the…formation of the Holy Roman Empire?"

"Correct. Thank you," Grier said, looking annoyed, and then moved on.

Thank you, Matt.

Heather turned to me and mouthed something that I was pretty sure was, "He can't hear you." I narrowed my eyes at her.

Are you going to help me find this narc or what?

Tap.

I was trying to figure out the best way to go about it and settled into thinking about my conversation with Heather the night of the party.

Hey, you said you hear some people better than others. Does that mean there are people you don't hear?

Tap, and, it seemed, some enthusiasm.

Maybe that's what you wanted to say before. You think the narc might be one of the people you can't hear.

Tap.

NIAC might be able to train their people…makes sense.

Tap.

"Heather? Do you know who I'm talking about?" Grier asked.

"Pope Clement the second," she answered, without hesitation.

"Yes, thank you."

Whose head did you pull that out of, Rob's? Isn't that against the rules?

She glared at me. And I almost laughed. *I'm not talking to you anymore. Pay attention. I'm just going to let all this marinate a while.*

Someone among us was a NIAC mole. That was huge. But I didn't have a way to find that out right now. The most I could do was warn any Talents I knew—and I didn't really know anyone except Kat and her friends. I was pretty sure I could count on Heather to spread the word, and we'd have to work on that threat later.

We. Jesus.

My immediate problem was Marco. Dylan was going to become a bank robber in two days if I didn't figure out what to do. Marco wasn't the narc, but he was a Talent. He had just as much to lose as the rest of us if someone had the kind of pictures of him that he had of Krista. I thought I could work with that.

* * *

Joss

"Um, yeah. I guess it would be a date."

"Jocelyn, you know how your father feels about you dating."

"That's why I'm asking you. Please? It's just pizza—at Donatello's, not the Pit. We won't be anywhere near the store, so Dad doesn't even have to know."

"Joss! Are you suggesting we lie to your father?"

"No, Mom, it's not like that, it's just...Look, I know Kat's party was a big disaster and that Dad wants me to stay away from her, and her friends, and...Dylan."

"And this boy, Eric, he's not part of that crowd?"

"No." *Lie.*

"You really like this boy?"

"I…" For some reason, I found it harder to lie about this part. I felt awful about having to lie to my mom and to play her like I was about to. It sucked. But it was when I got to the point of lying about which boy I liked that I balked? *Stupid brain.* "I know that I'm not like other kids. But sometimes I just want to pretend like I am."

"Aw, honey." Mom pulled me into her arms and I felt so bad I almost cried. "You're such a good girl. I know you try so hard to make things easier for Dad and me. You're such a help to us. I don't want to have to tell you no."

"Then don't. Just let me go and have this one afternoon. I don't really think anything's going to come of it. I know I can't really have a boyfriend. I just want to know what it feels like—to be normal."

My mom pulled back, brushed her lower lashes with her fingertips and blinked a few times. Then she sighed. "At least I don't have to worry if you can take care of yourself if he gets out of line."

I laughed, relieved. This was going to work. "Don't you hate it when those chair legs just break, all sudden-like?"

Mom laughed too. "Just make sure you're home before your dad and don't make me worry. Now, what are you going to wear? Should we do something with your hair?"

* * *

Dylan

"Hey man, guess what I'm doing." Eric said, as soon as I picked up.

"I can hear the wind, so I guess you're driving. I'm afraid to ask what it is or who it belongs to."

Marco had gotten us cell phones, the cash-only kind with no names attached. I think this enhanced his self-image as a crime boss. I had thought about flushing the damned thing, but I didn't want to piss him off right now. The night before I had dreamt that the whole grocery store job was just a way to trap me in the store and call the cops. Eric, it seemed, was embracing the convenience.

"Ha ha. It's my car. I'm on my way to pick up your girlfriend."

"Why? From where?" I was getting so used to people calling Joss my girlfriend I was forgetting to argue or pretend I didn't know who they were talking about. I was also forgetting that I didn't have the right to be so unreasonably pissed off at Eric's news.

"From her house, and I don't know why, actually. Kat grabbed me after school and asked me if I'd give her a ride somewhere later and got my number. She just called and told me I had to go pick up Joss at her house and then I'm supposed to go get Kat. She wouldn't tell me where they're going or what's up, though. She was just really particular about me getting Joss first, even though Kat's house is closer. Girls, man. I got no clue. But you want me to swing by and pick you up?"

Something was definitely up. Something Joss could have let me in on if she'd wanted to. What the hell was that about? What did I have to do to get this girl to trust me?

"Hey, what did you say? I think the connection's going."

Maybe I was supposed to trust her first.

"No. No thanks. I got some stuff to do right now. But do me a favor and call me when you get where you're going. Maybe I can hook up with you guys later."

"Yeah, ok. Later."

Eric clicked off, leaving me wondering, *Joss, what the hell are you up to?*

* * *

Joss

"So wait, I don't get it," Kat said, trying to keep her curls from blowing around. "How are we going to do this? Why did you send Eric away? We're going to need him."

We were standing in the middle of a construction zone, inside a skeleton of steel beams that would someday be some kind of conference center and pricey lunch spot overlooking the river. Right now it didn't look like much. Not to Kat. To me it looked like opportunity.

But I was as scared as I had ever been. More scared, maybe, than I had been at Kat's party. Then, everything had happened so fast that I didn't have time to feel it, I didn't have the luxury of thinking things over, and now I could tell myself that I couldn't be held completely responsible for my decisions.

This was totally different. This was a carefully thought-out plan—well, as carefully planned as it could be in the less than twenty-four hours I'd been working on it. I told myself I had to try now so there would still be time for a plan B if something went wrong. But really, I just wasn't giving myself time to chicken out.

Now I had come to the first irreversible step and I had to stop asking myself whether or not I really trusted Kat and just take the leap.

"We don't need Eric. I don't want anyone else involved."

"So you know how to hot-wire a crane?"

"You mean that crane?" I concentrated on it, on manipulating the safety devices that locked it in place. And then BOOM, the crane's arm plummeted from its raised position.

I caught it, moved it back up and locked it in place again. The giant magnet swung wildly on its cable. Kat was staring at me with giant cartoon eyes, and I was a little dizzy myself.

"Ooops. Maybe we should just…skip the crane. I'm not licensed."

"Did you really…?"

"Here's what we'll do…" I focused on a pile of beams at the edge of the worksite. One of them began to work itself up above the rest and hovered there while I refocused. Damn was it heavy. Maybe the heaviest thing I had tried to lift and that worried me. I raised it up several feet in the air and dropped it, catching it before it hit the pile again.

Kat gasped.

"I meant to do that."

I tried it a few more times, raising it, letting it go, catching it. Getting a feel for it. But I was getting tired. I set it down and rubbed at my temples.

"That was freakin' amazing, Joss!"

"Um, thanks."

"I mean really, seriously, like—wow! I can't believe you can do that. I mean, I just can't believe that you… Oh my God, you are such a faker! All that talk about me not being cautious with my Talent—"

"Hey, that's why you're here now."

"—and all that time it never occurred to you to say, 'Hey, by the way, I can move shit with my *brain'*? What kind of friend are you?"

I could see by her face that she thought she was funny. "In case you haven't noticed, I'm not real comfortable with the sharing."

"Really?" she snorted and then we were both quiet for a few minutes.

I pondered what I had just done. It was the first time I had ever showed my power to someone who wasn't family—on purpose anyway—since before the fire. What did that mean? Was that because of Kat and who she was, the way she had swooped into my life and made me her friend? Or did it have something to do with me, and how I was changing? Because I was…changing.

"Joss," Kat said, interrupting my thoughts.

"Yeah."

"You totally owe me a kitchen."

* * *

Dylan

I had been pacing my room with the phone in my hand for the last half hour. I should have just told Eric to pick me up before. I could have confronted Joss right then, and then I wouldn't be standing around here like an idiot wondering what she was up to. "Yeah?"

"Hey man." The background noise made it sound like Eric was still driving around.

"Where are you?"

"Um, ok, intense much? So the girls just wanted a ride. That's it. Then they told me to get lost. Can you believe that?"

"Well, where'd you take them?"

"You know the Riverfront Development thing? The big conference center project? Kat made me drop them near there."

"At the construction site?"

"Near there, yeah."

"And you just left them there?"

"Well since that's what they *wanted*, yeah. I mean, I thought I made it obvious I wanted to hang, but, you know, I wasn't about to *beg.*"

"Yeah yeah yeah. So what are they doing? When are you supposed to go back?"

"Dude, you need to chill. Who knows what they're doing. Use a guy for his wheels and then it's 'See ya!' So anyways, I'm free. You wanna do something?"

What the hell were they up to? At a construction site? I pretty much hated the idea of Joss—and Kat—out there by themselves. Because the longer I sat here alone and thought about it, the more I was sure she was up to something stupid. I thought about the picture I had given her at lunch and what I suspected. That kind of power might be a match even for Marco. Then I thought about him pawing at her out in the courtyard the other day and how she didn't do anything to stop it. Did she have the Talent or not? Would she even be willing to use it if she needed to?

"Hellllooooooo? Dude, you still there?"

"Yeah. Listen, I need you to swing by and pick me up. I need a ride."

He made a disgusted noise. "Eric's taxi service, coming up."

* * *

Joss

"You rang?" Marco asked as he crossed the concrete toward me. "So what's up, Joss? Why are we meeting out here? It's too early for my surprise birthday party." I was standing right where I wanted him, so I let him come all the way up to me, finger the collar of my jacket. "You must have thought more about my offer. Was this the only place you could think of to be alone? I've got someplace better and it's actually not too far away. Come on."

166

He tugged at my jacket, and I took a few steps back, breaking his hold and putting my hands up defensively. My heart was starting to beat hard, and I couldn't remember what I had planned to say. This was possibly the most important—and most dangerous—thing I had ever done. Had I planned to act nervous or was that just me?

"Thanks for coming but...I...just want to talk, ok?"

"What have we got to talk about? Please don't tell me you called me here to ask for favors, Joss." He was faking a whine, sounding pained. It was really annoying and helping me focus a bit. "I've got something you need: my silence. You need to give me something in return for that. It's that simple. Plus, baby, I got other stuff you need if you would just—"

"Can we not go there? I'm asking you one more time to be reasonable."

"I can't believe you dragged me all the way down here for this crap."

Above us was the sound of metal scraping against metal. The thought flashed through my mind: *when he thinks back, will he realize that I was looking up before it fell?*

Then I was screaming his name, running backward, getting out of the way as the beam plunged through space. Inside my head though, everything was calm, focused, concentrating on the moment when I might have to save him if he wasn't fast enough—or strong enough—to save himself.

He threw up his hands defensively and the beam landed. It was so wrong, like something out of a cartoon. There was a bend of his knees, a slight sinking of his body into a weight-lifter's stance as he took the weight. Then he was straightening, holding the huge steel girder above his head, and looking straight at me.

"What the fuck, Joss?" And he tossed it at me.

Shocked, I shrieked and stumbled backward, falling and landing on my butt in the dirt surrounding the concrete pour that was now cracked and gouged. I could have blocked it, I realized belatedly. I could have caught it and tossed it back to him. We could have made a game of it just to see who would tire first. But he had made me panic, and besides, he needed to be the star of this video.

"Oops," he said. "I guess it slipped. It's heavy."

"Um, yeah. It looks heavy," I agreed, getting up and brushing off dust. I raised my voice. "What do you think, Kat? You think that was heavy? Hey, did you get all that?"

The door to the construction office trailer opened and Kat walked down the few steps, regal as a queen, with her girl-scarf fluttering in the breeze from the river and a video camera held in front of her.

"Oh, heck yeah!" she called, watching the screen as she strolled toward us. "You guys should see the replay. It's awesome. Why Marco, what big muscles you have!"

"What the fuck?"

"I want to be sure you understand this, Marco, so I'll try to talk slowly and use small words." Cheesy movie line? Yes. But I was having a moment. "There is nothing worse than a person who destroys others' lives for personal gain—except someone who does it by throwing his own to the wolves. You've been blackmailing Talents and getting them hauled off by NIAC—and *you're* a Talent, you piece of shit. I don't understand how you could *do* that. To your own kind! And you know what? I don't even care. Because now we've got evidence. So you can back up off of Kat, my sister, Dylan—just keep your mouth shut. Because if anything happens to us, or if we hear of you threatening any other Talents again, that video goes straight to NIAC."

"Yeah. And the local news, and anyone else we can think of." Kat added. She was almost to the edge of the concrete on the other side of what would become the lobby, when her ankle turned in her impractical shoe and she looked down to right herself.

And that's when Marco went for her. I knew then that I hadn't thought this through and there was no time now.

"Kat! Run!"

She turned and fled, leaving the shoe, and Marco caught up to her fast. I raced toward them, but he was on the point of reaching for the scarf that fluttered behind her. I was close, but not close enough to a guy who could break her in half like a twig. I did the only thing in my head, I took a nearby pallet of lumber and slid it between them.

Marco skidded to a halt and crashed into the pile anyway. Wooden posts spilled down the stack, as he pushed himself up again, and I tackled him.

CHAPTER 18

Joss

Oh my God, ow.

That's what I thought about my ill-conceived flying tackle at Marco that slammed us both hard against the stacked lumber. We slid down, losing our footing some, and then, before I stopped feeling the zinging shock of the impact through my arm and shoulder, he was already shoving me off him.

Damn, he could shove. I planted my foot, focusing the air behind me into a temporary wall that would keep me from falling on my ass again. His face was a mask of rage as he lead with a punch that was designed to take me in the face and level me. But, like my dad had taught me, I stepped offline and grabbed his arm as it whizzed by my head. I pulled hard, using the incredible momentum that came with the awesome power behind his punch to yank him off balance.

He went stumbling forward. He should have fallen flat from that move; physics should have made sure of it. But he had the same kind of super strength in his lower body that he had in his brawler's chest and arms, and when he planted his foot, it stayed planted. He pivoted on it, turning back to face me.

"I don't care what you can do with your Talent, you bitch, I'm getting that camera. You can step off and I'll go after Kat, or you can let me pound on you, which I'll enjoy, and then I'll get her. Your choice."

It's not like I was standing there doing nothing during the moment it took him to deliver this speech. I was reassessing, getting the lay of the land. Figuring out what I could use. All the good stuff was too far away, so I reached out with my mind for one of the wooden posts on the top of the stack and brought it down on his head for an answer.

Marco's arm arced through the air and practically sliced through the wood. It broke in half, and I turned my face away to avoid any splinters. That's when he came at me with his fists.

This was nothing like sparring with my dad in the woods, learning how to duck, weave, and use my Talent in a fight. No matter how hard we trained, it always came down to the fact that we really didn't want to damage each other. We were both holding back. And even though Dad could sometimes be scary, I realized that I had never known what scared really was until Marco came after me with murder in his eyes.

He was holding nothing back, slugging at me with a barroom brawl style of alternating punches that came too fast to dodge them all. But time was slowing, nothing but the moment-to-moment punches and blocks. My mind was working even harder than my body, concentrating on focusing the air around my fists to maximize my own impact. To me it felt like punching a fragile balloon, feeling the pop of the air dissipating before my fist struck flesh. To him, it would feel like I'd hit him with a block of wood before my bloodied knuckles made contact. Even harder for me, probably because they were more important, were the cushions of air I formed to block his blows. It was all that kept him from punching right through me. He was past the point now of looking confused at the feeling of punching into a bag of water before he made contact with me. Now he was concentrating too, on trying to hit me so hard I wouldn't be able to protect myself.

I was letting him drive me back across the site, back toward the more active part of the work area where all the heavy stuff was. It was getting harder and harder to concentrate, harder to keep raising my arms to hit back, and the pain from even his muffled blows was starting to cut through the adrenaline. I knew that I was now fighting for my life and if I dropped, if I slipped, it was over. Panic started to nibble at the ends of my concentration and I started to feel desperate. I had to find some way to end this.

From the corner of my eye I could finally see the dumpster. It was a huge, construction project container that might hold him—at least long enough for me to get away and hide for a few moments. If I could just regroup, get closer to something I could do damage with… I ducked to the side, unexpectedly disengaging and gaining just a moment to turn my gaze toward it.

It shot up in the air, flipped over, littering the site with a trail of building scraps as it sailed toward us.

Marco's fist connected with my kidney and, even though I saw it coming, even though I automatically tried to save myself, it was like being hit by a car. I felt the hideous pain of impact, felt my body go airborne, heard the dumpster crash to the ground a moment before I did. I skidded in dirt, heard the tearing of my sleeve, but didn't feel my body stop before the black at the edges of my vision took everything over.

A heavy slap, like a bear with its dinner, brought me around. So much pain knifed its way through my head that I wasn't even sure where it was coming from. Marco loomed above me, his features twisted with hatred and satisfaction as his hands closed around my throat.

So that's it, then.

That's what my last thought was going to be, knowing that he could snap my neck and that he wanted to. But that had been almost a minute ago. In this minute, with me trapped beneath him, my arms pinned at my sides by his legs, Marco wanted to squeeze.

* * *

Dylan

"This is where I left the girls. They said they were going to go down to the river. Let's go down and check it out."

"Yeah, ok."

Eric had picked up on the fact that I was really freaking out, but when I cut off his questions, he hadn't pressed me. He drove like a maniac to get back over here, but we had hit rush hour and it seemed like no one was in any hurry to get home. Every minute I was beating myself up about not going with them earlier because, somehow, I knew something was wrong.

That's what I was thinking about when Kat came tearing through the tree line in a limping run, her hair a wreck, one shoe gone, looking absolutely terrified. We called out and raced toward her but she didn't slow down until she had me by the jacket and was shaking me and talking way too fast.

Eric came around behind her, wrapped his arms around her, separated us. "Slow down, Kat. We can't understand you. Just take a breath."

"Where is Joss, Kat? What happened?" I demanded.

"She—Marco—help her!"

"Where?"

Eric had loosened his hold, and Kat panted, "At the construction site. I think he's gonna kill her." She pointed back the way she had come, turning, but as soon as she took a step her ankle folded and she started to go down. Eric caught her.

"I got this. Go on," I heard him say, but I was already racing through the trees.

They seemed so far off when I saw them, and even though I was running all out, it wasn't fast enough. They were two dark-haired figures trading savage blows, and I couldn't believe one of them was Joss, taking him on like that.

She dodged and blocked like a professional fighter. Looking at Marco, I could see he wasn't holding back, and that he was driving her backward across the site. He was landing blows that should have knocked her on her ass, worse, but she just kept going. Still I was terrified, thinking that he must be holding something back, he must be, and soon he'd get tired of playing with her...

She dodged, moving out of the fight and turning, leaving herself open. Nearby, a huge dumpster shot up and flipped over as it whizzed toward them. Then it suddenly fell, bouncing once in the dirt and my eyes shot back to the fight.

Joss's body was just coming to a skidding halt several feet from where they'd been fighting. Her body went limp. It was a moment where the whole world seemed to stop, as if it just couldn't keep going, and yet it was. Even my legs were still moving as if everything but my mind knew that the world was still turning.

Marco fell on her, straddling her body with his knees on either side of her chest. He slapped her hard across the face. I felt a fresh burst of rage as he struck her, and on its heels a nearly overwhelming relief to see her move beneath him. Then his hands wrapped around her throat and relief and hope were obliterated by the return of panic.

I didn't stop to yell at him, I just poured what little speed I had left into my sprint, pushed off from the ground, and launched myself at him.

* * *

Joss

It was a streak of moving air and dark colors that knocked Marco aside and brought oxygen back to my world again. For the barest instant I thought maybe I had done it, that in my last moments my mind had gathered the last of its power to reach out and find a weapon to save me. But as my head fell limply to the side I saw two bodies rolling in dirt. And when they separated, as they gained their feet, I saw that it was Dylan, covered in dust, and taking a quick step back from Marco, planting his feet and raising his fists.

Dylan. Bent on suicide.

"You sure you wanna do this, buddy?" Marco asked derisively.

"I'm going to fucking kill you."

"How're you gonna do that? Come on, Dylan. Give it up. We've been friends a long time, and I can use a guy like you. You know that. Let's not do this. Not over a girl. Especially not over that girl."

Dylan's fist flew. It connected with Marco's face hard enough to send Marco stumbling back. They both stood there for an instant, stunned. Then Marco retaliated, a blow we all knew should have knocked Dylan out into the middle of next week. Without thinking I threw up a block, as though I'd been trained for it the way I'd been trained to protect myself. Marco's swing hesitated as it hit my block, and by the time it actually pushed through, Dylan had dodged the worst of it. It hardly phased him.

"Fucking bitch," I heard Marco say as Dylan's gaze flicked my way, questioning.

And then they were in it.

They circled each other, trading a series of quick blows. Dad had made me watch a lot of fights on TV, teaching me about telegraphing and what to look for, and it was just like that. From back here I could see nearly everything Marco was going to do before he did it, and throw up a wall to protect Dylan from the worst of it. I didn't have it in me to pelt him with rocks or fly in even so much as a stout stick to help out. But by absorbing the force of Marco's supernatural blows with my own Talent, I could make it more of an even fight between two boys who were really pissed.

I couldn't lend any more force to Dylan's punches, but I didn't have to. He was just whaling on the guy he was still calling his best friend a few days ago. He was taking some hard hits; I could tell he felt them from the way his body reacted, but he shrugged off the blows and kept coming back, harder.

They didn't speak to each other. There were no sounds but the scrape of dirt under boots, the thuds of flesh hitting flesh, and the grunts that accompanied. The sound of the blood pounding in my head as I fought through the pain to stay in it too, knowing that if I couldn't help Dylan, it would be over for both of us.

On and on they fought, with time stretching out, every punch I tried to block feeling like a giant screw turning in my skull, and every hit Dylan took feeling like a knock to my own heart until I almost couldn't breathe. I promised I'd let myself cry about it later, when I was alone, if I could just stay with it a little bit longer...

They were both wearing down, hurting. Marco was starting to weave, and I could actually see the moment when Dylan realized it, a new determination washing his features, and a new energy in his next attack. A few quick jabs and then he landed a vicious blow to the side of Marco's head, one that whipped it sideways. Marco staggered away, righted himself. Spat blood. Dylan stepped in with a savage gut punch that drove Marco to one knee, gasping for air.

Marco clutched his middle, breathing in ragged, shallow pants. Dylan could end it now. Another head shot from that angle would put Marco out. But he stood there, fists still raised, waiting.

"You broke my goddamned ribs," Marco wheezed. "I can't believe what a fucking traitor you turned out to be. I've called you my best friend my whole life and you turn on me for a chick. A freak chick. God *damn* you!"

"I didn't turn on you, Marco. You turned on me when you decided you owned me. When you decided that what you couldn't get by playing on our friendship, you should try to get with threats and intimidation. You're out of control, and it's not just about Joss or me, it's Rob, Krista, Kat—everyone and anyone else you've tried to destroy. You've got to be stopped."

"And you think you're the one to do it? You think you can stand in my way?"

"I should have tried, a long time ago. Maybe if I had stood up to you years ago you wouldn't be who you are now."

"Puh-leez. Don't overestimate yourself."

"What I'm finally finished doing is overestimating you. You're not even capable of being a human being anymore and I'm done."

Marco pushed back to his feet, pale and holding onto his ribs. He swayed and then steadied.

"No you're not. I'm just getting started, and you're going to find that you can either do things my way, or this is just going be round one, and next time—"

"You wanna go for round two right now?"

"You'd like that, wouldn't you? Don't think a few broken ribs or that stupid video changes anything," he said, turning slightly to include me in the conversation for the first time. "I'm gonna own this town and everyone in it. And it's gonna happen sooner than you think."

"How did you get so completely deluded?" I asked, trying to get enough venom into it that I wouldn't sound so weak.

He actually grinned, showing a mouthful of bloody teeth. "Time will tell, won't it?" He wheezed out a cough, began to back away, then just turned and started to limp off.

I watched Dylan gather his reserves of strength and take the first few steps to follow. Hadn't he had enough? He had to be punch drunk crazy. "Dylan," I called, even though it hurt to take in enough air to make myself heard. I was so scared he wasn't going to hear me or wasn't going to listen to reason.

The next moment he was kneeling beside me, yanking me into his arms so fast the world grayed again.

"Ow!"

I'll admit I had fantasized about Dylan's fingers in my hair but...

"No blood," he said, looking at his hand. "Your pupils look about the same size, that's a thing, right?"

That would be the *him staring into my eyes* part.

"How many fingers?"

"Would you leave me alone? I'm fine." At his doubtful look I added, "Mostly. What about you?" I wanted to reach out to touch him, but, yeah, head injury or no, I just didn't have the guts for that. Something inside my head was wanting to replay the whole scene and point out how Dylan had charged to my rescue. Which I think explained why I kept wanting to faint. And since that was too girly to contemplate, I knocked that something around until it shut up.

"I'm ok. A couple bruises. Nothing cracked, nothing broken. I can't believe how—"

"Yeah," I interrupted. "I can't believe he held back like that. In the end I guess your friendship meant more to him than we thought."

Dylan gave me a searching look. I wondered if he could guess that I'd been protecting him, or if there was any hope he'd buy the *Marco's Mercy* angle. You'd think by that time I would have totally trusted him. Maybe I did. Maybe it was just that I didn't want him to know I was a freak. Not for sure. Or maybe it was just habit.

"You scared the crap out of me," he told me. His demeanor had changed. His voice was lower, slower. He was stroking his thumb against my cheek for no reason I could figure out, and even looking at me differently, like softly, but still intense. His eyes dropped to my mouth. "I can't believe you took him on like that. What were you thinking?"

I was thinking about you.

I couldn't say it. I couldn't breathe.

Then my eyes fell closed when his mouth touched mine. Brushed, then lightly pressed. I had no idea a kiss would feel like this. The world seemed to tilt and everything slid away. There was nothing but Dylan, his arm around me, the hand that cupped my face, the hardness of his chest, and the crazy beat of his heart under my hand. The incredible softness of his lips as they moved against mine.

A car horn made us both jump, and we saw Eric's car bouncing across the dirt. That explained how Dylan had found us. And if they'd started looking where Eric had dropped us before, he would have had to drive all the way around the trees that bordered the southern side of the site. The car braked and Kat jumped out, stumbled, and caught herself on the door. Then she hurried, a bit more carefully, toward us.

"Oh my God, is she ok?"

At that point I think I was more likely to die from embarrassment and confusion than from any injury.

"I'm fine. Worry about Rambo here. He's the one who came racing to my rescue and beat on Marco until he went home in tears."

Dylan snorted. "That's not exactly how it happened. And we theorize he was going easy on me."

Kat looked from me to Dylan and back, her eyes narrowed.

"Anyway," he continued, "we were trying to decide if Joss has a concussion and should go to the hospital. I vote hospital."

"Seconded!" by Kat.

"Vetoed," by me. "Look, guys. You know I can't do that. My dad…"

"Hey, here's your shoe," Eric said, joining us. "Joss, how many shoes am I holding up?"

"One sorry excuse for footwear that almost got this girl killed. I knew those things were dangerous. Let me up."

"This is probably the point where we berate you for your idiot plan that you didn't us tell about," Dylan said, more or less lifting me to my feet. The world grayed a little, but then things brightened up again.

"Save it for later. Please."

"I still think you should go to the hospital."

"Here Joss, take this." Eric grabbed my hand and slapped a cell phone into it. "We'll take her home, she'll go to bed, and you can call her every hour to make sure she knows her name and who's President or whatever. That's what they do in the hospital anyway, right?"

"I guess the opportunity to berate you hourly will give me some satisfaction."

I have to admit that I was pretty overwhelmed at this point. Kat had the video that was going to protect us from any more of Marco's threats. My sister's secret was safe, and with it, my dad's sanity. I'd gone up against my own kind, Talent *y* Talent, so to speak. I'd picked one who was meaner and stronger than I was and had managed to come out the other side.

Ok, so I'd gotten involved with people and it almost ended in disaster. I'd used my Talent in front of others twice now and it almost ended in disaster. But it didn't. I'd made things better. Using my ability had helped save Phil, Kat, my sister…

And Dylan had kissed me, which I wasn't even going to let myself contemplate for a while.

All that would have been enough, but there was something in particular that was really blowing my mind when Kat hugged me as we made our way through the construction dust to Eric's car.

I was among friends.

I felt like they were, and more, that I wanted them to be. I was still nervous, unsure and unused to it. But that day I knew that I wanted people in my life, and it didn't matter if that would obligate me to help them, because maybe I wanted that too. Maybe I wanted to save the world, I don't know. Maybe I was high on victory. Maybe it was just the endorphins doing my thinking.

I slid into the car and Dylan slid in next to me. Closer than he needed to so that it would be so easy to lean my aching head against his shoulder. I let it fall back instead, unsure of how to act. We were all tired. I had serious mixed feelings at the thought of a phone vibrating under my pillow every hour all night, even if he would be on the other end of it.

"You don't really need to call me. It's nice of you to offer, but I'll be fine."

"I'm calling you."

"No, really. Don't."

"Joss, you might have just stopped Marco and saved me from a life of crime," he said, easing his arm around me so my head rested on his shoulder, "and don't think I don't appreciate it, but...

"You are so not the boss of me."

THE END

Can't get enough Teen Paranormal Romance? Try these great indie authors…

Stacey Wallace Benefiel- The *Zellie Wells Trilogy* provides readers with fun, relatable teen characters, surprising storylines, and a fresh take on psychic ability. The innocent sensuality of the love story in the first volume, *Glimpse,* makes for a memorable read in ebook and paperback. The sequel, *Glimmer,* is expected in Autumn 2010, with *Glow* to follow in Summer 2011. http://staceywb.webs.com

Imogen Rose- With a hint of sci-fi edge, the *Portal Chronicles* series makes a mom into a mad scientist, trying to use time-travel to create her perfect life. Caught up in the experiment is Arizona, a hockey-star tomboy who finds herself plunked down in an alternate reality that belongs to a Barbie doll, cheerleader version of herself. *Portal,* and *Equilibrium* are available in ebook and paperback. *Quantum* is expected to release on October 31, 2010. http://imogenrose.com

Like Paranormal Romance with adult characters? Here are some other indie favs...

Kait Nolan- Kait's *Mirus* series provides a perfect blend of romance and action, set in a paranormal world that bumps up against our own. A fresh mythology and fast-paced writing leave the reader breathless and wanting more. *Forsaken by Shadow* is currently available as an ebook, with other Mirus stories expected in late 2010. http://kaitnolan.com

Zoe Winters- In her *Preternaturals* series, Zoe brings life to the undead and other magical beings with imagination, sensuality, and humor. Interconnected novellas Kept, Claimed, and Mated are currently available separately as ebooks. A compilation volume, Blood Lust, is available in both ebook and print versions. http://zoewinters.org

COME FIND ME!

Here are some places where I post news and information, and generally hang out...

Website and Blog:
http://susan-bischoff.com

Twitter:
http://twitter.com/susan_bischoff

Facebook:
http://facebook.com/pages/Susan-Bischoff/137550366285624

MySpace:
http://www.myspace.com/susan-bischoff

Goodreads:
http://www.goodreads.com/author/show/4171164.Susan_Bischoff

Email:
susanbischoff@gmail.com

Made in the USA
Charleston, SC
12 March 2011